The Fallen

By Melissa Barker-Simpson

Copyright © 2015

Acknowledgements

I'm fortunate to belong to a wonderful writing community; valued friends and colleagues who, like a fountain of endless support, encourage and inspire me to give a voice to the characters in my head.

Each novel brings its own challenges. This time it was finding the right cover to reflect Maddison and her power. Kathryn Jenkins came to the rescue, and I cannot thank her enough for her creation, or her patience.

I would also like to extend my appreciation to Louise Findlay; an inspiring young woman who shares my passion for language. We have had many conversations about the world I created within the Fractured, and her love of poetry influenced a description or two in this story.

There are also those who work incredibly hard behind the scenes, those who provide a second pair of eyes and help to ensure the work is at its best. I must therefore acknowledge the support and guidance of my editor, David Burton. Thank you, Dave, for being my sounding board, and for catching the things I missed.

Last, and by no means least, to my readers. Thank you for loving the characters as I do, and for taking the journey with me.

Also by Melissa Barker-Simpson

Fractured Series

The Contract (Prequel) – Part of the double book anthology: Changing Worlds

Worlds Apart Series

The Fifth Watcher (Book 1)

Morgan and Fairchild Series

Sins of the Father (Book 1)

Hands of Evil (Book 2)

Gifted Series

The Conduit (Book 1)

The Missing Link (Book 2)

Writing under Nat Hobson

Winchester Brothers Series

Addy's Choice (Book 1)

Heart of Fire (Book 2)

PROLOGUE

Zara had prepared for this moment for centuries, explored the endless possibilities of her new role – for the Fall. It was a privilege to be chosen. A gift. Yet she was nervous. A deep cavern had formed in her chest; a sense of knowing she couldn't quite reach.

Perhaps it was the unfamiliar chambers in which she now sat. In the mortal realm, it would be a receiving room of sorts; a waiting area when Zara had no patience to wait.

Her attention drifted, her gaze roaming the chamber, exploring the smooth, clean surfaces. The seating area bordered the room in a wide semi-circle, set back from a dial shaped alter in the centre. Zara felt both curious and afraid of the intricate symbols marring the gentle curves. They were harsh, foreign even, and anxiety quickened in her stomach.

"Why so glum, Zara the Fair?"

Looking up, Zara watched Lucas cross the room; his abrupt arrival signalling an end to the waiting. He had a knowing look on his face, one Zara had seen in the light of his eyes since childhood. The energy which swirled around them, turning the calm into a chaotic storm of emotion, was the only chance they would get to say goodbye. Zara would miss her dear friend, though they would meet again.

"Glum, Lucas?" Zara's amusement quelled the tension. "You spend too much time with mortals."

"And yet, you are the one who will fall. Not I." His powerful light, the essence of him, flared bright. Evidence of his own good humour.

"Is it time?"

Her brothers and sisters had already joined the ranks of the Fallen. Even now they awaited her arrival, ready to assist the transition on Earth.

"As impatient as ever, I see." Lucas took Zara's hand and led her to the alter. "Will you miss being a Guardian?"

She thought about his question, smiling when she found the answer he would appreciate. "Once a Guardian, always a Guardian."

Lucas' laughter enveloped her, a play of red in the sea of blue. "I will enjoy watching you learn and grow. I haven't had this much fun since your early days of training."

It wasn't the whole truth. He would miss the teasing, miss the subtle ways Zara led him astray. Lucas was far too serious. It was not his only flaw.

Glancing down at the dial, Zara followed the movement as it opened wide like a giant mouth. It revealed only darkness, the edge of nothing she was supposed to embrace as part of the process.

Lucas bent to place his forehead against hers. "Be well, Zara the Fair."

Panic bubbled again, threatening Zara's composure. "What happens now?"

"Now?" Lucas grinned, his azure blue eyes twinkling with a mischief she rarely saw. "Now you fall." He leaned in close to Zara's ear. "You can do this. Just...let go."

ONE

It was deathly quiet within the outskirts of the city, but then the rats hiding in the shadows were no ordinary rats. After the Demonic War, London had lost some of its glamour, and now people knew their nightmares were real they rarely ventured from the centre.

Demons still lurked in the smaller towns, and, like hangers-on after a concert, they refused to leave. For the most part, mercenaries took care of the problem; freelance hunters who followed their own laws. Maddison Wood was one such mercenary, or she had been before she accepted a position with the Race Alliance and was appointed to the Legion of Watchers – the first time in history the position was afforded to a witch.

Tonight she was off duty, or she should have been. Something had drawn her to the capital, and she always followed her instincts. Those instincts were screaming at her, drowning out the voice in her head. She stilled, eyes on alert, senses attuned to any sign of foul play. Something big was coming. She could smell it, like the stench of evil had permeated the very streets.

"What is it?" Donovan asked, turning in a slow circle.

"Damned if I know," she muttered, moving again. "I feel...something."

Donovan's gaze swung her way. "I really don't like the sound of that."

Maddison shrugged, unable to put her fear into words. He didn't expect her to. Their connection bypassed such necessity. If she said they were meant to be there, he didn't question it.

In the past year, Donovan had become her shadow, or as she preferred to call him, a Class-A side-kick. He'd rarely left her side since she had won his contract in a fight for his honour. The Hympe Trials, a prerequisite for Donovan's kind, and a hundred years in length, were meant as a form of transition. The system was often abused, so when she had found him, broken and helpless in a demon cell, she couldn't walk away. His term was almost up, and he had more than earned his freedom.

"Oh, you've got to be kidding me," Maddison groaned, hackles rising.

"What?"

She didn't look Donovan's way, her eyes were glued to the street, to the ball of light which glowed like a beacon of tightly controlled power. "Orion Reece," she said through clenched teeth.

'*Am I supposed to know who that is?*' Donovan asked, his voice a deep rumble inside her mind.

She could feel his eyes on her, but she didn't turn.

When Orion appeared, he did so with none of the arrogance she had come to expect, and, for some reason, the lack of drama unnerved her more than his presence. He was a god, one who enjoyed flaunting his superiority every chance he got. The pale blonde hair, hanging to his shoulders like fine silk, still shone as a testament to his power, and yet alarm bells were ringing in Maddison's head. Something was definitely wrong with the picture.

"To what do we owe the pleasure?" she asked, her voice and gaze steady. She would not give him an inch.

"Come now, Woody." His dark eyes flashed, the gold at the outer edges drawing her in. "You can do better than that."

'*Woody?*' Donovan asked through their connection.

'*Long story*,' Maddison replied. She took a step towards Orion, delighted when Donovan followed suit.

"We haven't been introduced," Donovan said, extending his hand.

Orion threw back his head and laughed. "My dear boy, if you want to know more about me, all you have to do is ask."

As a hympe, Donovan had a unique gift. It was empathy based, so if he opened himself up to the connection, he could learn anything through touch.

"I'll forgive the discourtesy," Orion continued. "Because I have you at a disadvantage." His eyes grew cold. "I'm the reason you current owner stumbled upon your sorry excuse for a-"

"Nobody owns him," Maddison said, stepping between them. "And you're not the only reason he's free."

Orion raised his hand, eyes flashing with challenge. Maddison's hair slithered towards him, the long braid dancing in the cool night air, like he was a regular snake charmer.

"Is that so?" he asked.

Maddison shot magic into the wayward locks and regained the advantage. She knew Orion used the trick to test her, to steal her control. Given that her hair was her weapon of choice, it was an effective reprimand.

'*What's he talking about?*' Donovan asked.

'He sent me to the Firmani Caves, or at least set it up so I would be in the right place at the right time.'

Donovan's shudder was involuntary. The Firmani Caves were home to the Nrikabat demons, the original proprietors of his contract – those responsible for his torture and abuse.

"How did you know?" Donovan asked, staring wide-eyed at Orion. "Why would you care?"

"I don't." Orion's tone was bored. "But I owed your father a favour."

'Don't listen to him,' Maddison said, touching Donovan with her mind. 'Even if he's telling the truth, he will use the information against you. I'll find another way to learn his secrets.'

She turned her attention to Orion. Everything about him was designed to entice - the tall, sculptured body, strong jaw, sinful mouth; he was quite a package. "Can we just get this over with? Why don't you tell us what you want?"

"Oh, how you wound me," he said, placing a hand over his heart. "Can't I have the simple desire to visit with an old friend?"

He was stalling, she realised. Taunting them purposely, perhaps hoping they would lose the trail. She could almost feel her instincts curling up in her gut, retreating into silence. "If you're here to shoot the breeze, we can do that as we walk," she said, starting to move past him.

Orion sidestepped, putting himself in her path. His strong jaw was set, lips pressed into a hard line. "You need to get as far away from here as possible," he said, his voice low and urgent.

She blinked, genuinely surprised by the concern in his dark eyes. "Something's coming, isn't it?"

There was a long beat of silence. "You don't want to get tangled up in this, Maddy." He squinted, assessing her reaction. "Don't force my hand."

Donovan moved so he was shoulder to shoulder with Maddison. "That sounds like a threat."

She almost smiled. Donovan had no idea who he was dealing with; either that or he had a death wish. Orion could squash him like a bug; though, granted, Donovan hadn't been crushed yet.

"If he was going to do something, he'd have done it already," she said. "He either can't interfere, or the focused use of his power will give him away." That was it. She knew it as soon as the words left her mouth. Why there had been no fanfare when he arrived, why the light of his power was subdued. "It's big, isn't it?" she said, more to herself than Orion, because she knew he wouldn't answer.

"Don't say I didn't warn you." He vanished before she could respond to the ominous warning, taking the light with him.

"Who the hell was that?" Donovan asked, staring into empty space.

"Some say he's Draco's right hand man, and a member of the Fractured." She let that hang between them for a moment. The Fractured were responsible for the Demonic War; their need for power a driving force. The group answered to no one but Draco, their fearless leader. Most believed he was the heart of darkness itself.

Donovan stepped into a stream of light, studying her face. His stormy grey eyes were probing. "What do you think?"

"I think Orion answers to no one unless it suits a need." She fingered the gold band around her neck. "I'm surprised you didn't recognise him." Donovan had taken her memories the day they met, saw things during the connection she shared with no one else.

She saw his eyes flicker to the necklace and linger there. "He didn't appear in any of your memories, though there is a shadow I cannot explain."

Maddison stared at him, more disturbed than surprised that Orion had protected their history somehow. "I met him during my captivity. He helped me to focus my power and disable the leash." Her fingers tapped on the metal at her neck. "I owed him for that, and I paid up in full."

They walked in silence for a while as Maddison thought of her imprisonment, of her brothers. Not her biological brothers, she was an only child. But they were family in all the ways that mattered. Maddison's childhood was a blur of painful memories. She had moved from one home to another in a perpetual state of terror until she discovered her powers and, finally, her freedom. She had been thirteen.

Within days of discovering her gift she had met a vampire; a warrior and protector of the race. Triston was the closest thing she had to a father. His son, Zachariah had resented her for years, but eventually they formed a relationship which was now bound in a thousand battles fought together. She had followed him into danger more than once, spent endless months in captivity trying to save his ass. It was how they met Michael.

They often joked about their friendship; the witch, the vampire and the elf. They were an unlikely trio and it worked. Michael was the worst affected by their imprisonment, and, when Maddison had returned him to his people, they had forged an even stronger bond. She hadn't left his side until he had returned; heart, body and soul.

Donovan nudged her with his elbow. "What are you thinking about?"

"Michael. I should visit him on my next day off." Maddison grinned at his sceptical expression. Today was a day off, and here they were – out looking for trouble. "It's different. Something is coming." Her eyes darted to the shadows. She could feel the energy humming along her skin. "Or maybe it's already here."

Donovan took a step closer, his presence a buffer against the dark. "Maybe you should call for backup," he said. "Where's Zachariah tonight?"

"He's on assignment with Sebastian." Though Zachariah was her partner, it was part of the job to give priority to their Charge. Sebastian, in her brother's case, needed him more than she did right now. "I want to see what I can shake loose, before I call in reinforcements."

"You say that as though you won't wade right into the action."

She bumped her shoulder against his. "It's lucky I have you then."

That got a grunt in response, which only made Maddison smile. They made a good team, so unless they stepped into a war zone, she wasn't worried about her chances.

***

"Holy shit." Obadiah slammed onto the concrete with enough force to break a dozen newly formed bones. He was as weak as a kitten and he didn't have a taste for it, or the blood filling his mouth. His power would not return until he'd been through the transition, which meant he was bound to the restrictions of his human body.

And the pain, dear god but it hurt like a bitch. He was as helpless as a new-born, and in some respects that's what he was.

He spit a wad of blood onto the pavement, surprised he had the energy. Not that it would do a damn bit of good against his enemies; he could barely turn his head.

As if on cue, he caught a glint of steel belonging to twin toe-caps and groaned in anticipation. The demon attached to the fancy boots kicked him hard, connecting with his shoulder and, thankfully, not his skull. Every blow shot a white-hot blast of pain along his spine. Obadiah was clenching his jaw so tight he was surprised it didn't break. At this rate it would be the only bone in his body still intact.

He had to bite down on a scream when scum-in-boots picked him up by his shirt; an impressive feat considering Obadiah's human form was six foot three and weighed two hundred and ten pounds.

The demon held him suspended as though he weighed no more than a kitten; waiting, though Obadiah had no idea for what. He got his answer a minute later; Obadiah felt the threat before he actually saw it.

He hadn't planned on meeting the Fractured so soon. But then his only priority had been finding a way into the mortal realm.

Obadiah squinted to focus his wavering vision. A section of the brick wall in front of him disappeared, or if not disappeared, it was obscured from view by the long, oblong shaped energy field forming before his eyes. The power required to conjure such a doorway meant only one thing. Whoever created it was a heavy hitter.

Of course it would be their leader. Why not?

Draco stepped into the side street as though he owned it. Obadiah had to blink to readjust to the darkness when the pale gold light of the doorway snuffed out. The oily, repugnant stench of Draco's malevolence was suffocating. If it hadn't been for the pallor of his skin, a chalky white, he would be one with the shadows that swirled around him. Draco's eyes were dark, bottomless pits, his hair the colour of a raven's wing.

The leader of the Fractured was the original lost soul, and he wore the darkness like a favoured coat. It was obvious he used his appearance to intimidate. He was tall, and broad, and content to be seen as a scary looking son of a bitch.

"Oh how the mighty have fallen," Draco said, bending slightly to meet Obadiah's gaze. "This is almost too easy."

"What can I say? I didn't think it through." Obadiah gritted his teeth against the pain in his neck. He wanted to let go, let his head fall forward, but he would never bow to the darkness. "I don't suppose you want to do this later. Say…in a day or two?"

Draco laughed, a cold sound which held no humour. "I'm afraid not. Your presence here puts a kink in my plans."

Obadiah swallowed hard. Draco's punishment would be brutal, it would make the welcome doled out by his two minions seem like child's play. Draco couldn't kill him, he didn't have the power, but he could certainly prevent Obadiah from fulfilling his own mission.

As though reading his thoughts, Draco snapped his fingers towards scum-in-boots and a second later had a sword in his hand.

"You know." Draco ran a finger along the blade, drawing blood. "I'm surprised someone with your power is this careless. Surely you knew an event of this magnitude would not go unchecked? You may as well be wearing a sign around your neck."

If I'd known, would I be hanging here, bleeding all over your shoes?

Obadiah resisted the urge to roll his eyes. "Poor timing." It was the truth, and he saw no reason to lie. The fact was, there hadn't been a choice. He was forbidden to enter the mortal realm in his true form, so out of desperation, or perhaps insanity, he had fallen.

"More like poor judgement." Draco lifted the sword above his head. "Say hello to your-"

A piercing whistle cut through Draco's words like a blade. His head snapped to the right, hunting the origin of the sound.

Obadiah turned, too, though it took him a little longer.

"Step away from the Fallen, Draco. He's under my protection." *What the hell?*

Obadiah squinted at the woman who seemed to blend into her surroundings like she had been carved from the darkness itself. Her waist-length hair was the colour of midnight and tamed into a long braid. She was clad in a tight, form fitting suit, which appeared elfin in nature. His gaze flicked to her braid when he realised the thing was twitching like a cat's tail. He couldn't see her face, not yet, it was encased in shadow. But there was something familiar about her. He knew this woman.

"Come on, Draco, you know the rules." Her voice ricocheted off the walls like the crack of a whip.

Obadiah turned to glance at Draco, surprised he hadn't vaporised her where she stood. The rage on Draco's face told him the pair had tangoed before.

The thought jogged a memory, a flash of blazing colour, and he knew. This was Maddison Wood.

Shit, what are the chances?

"I'll give you three seconds to back your pretty little ass up," Draco said, lowering the sword slowly. "Three, two…" A burst of white hot energy shot from the sword. "One."

Maddison blocked the attack. She had a shield in her hand, an odd-looking construct. It was transparent, except for a ring of gold. As Draco's power hit the shield it bounced back in their direction. Instead of hitting Draco it went wide, severing the arm of scum-in-boots. Obadiah dropped to the concrete like a sack of skin and bone.

He flipped onto his back, wincing when scum-in-boots screeched like a banshee. It earned him a direct hit from Draco's sword. Clearly he had a low tolerance for noise. Either that or he had something against banshees.

Maddison didn't even miss a beat. She threw her shield at Draco, which was when Obadiah realised it wasn't a shield at all. It was a large ring. It expanded in the air, dropping to the ground to form a circle around Draco.

Obadiah flinched when a wall of flame shot up from the centre, engulfing Draco, who screamed; more in frustration than pain.

The flame snuffed out in the next instant, but Maddison was prepared. She flicked her wrist and the ring rose from the ground, shrinking to bind Draco's hands to his sides.

It's a distraction.

Obadiah glared at the demon who hurried across to him. He blended so well into the shadows, Obadiah almost missed him. He didn't know if it was the way the demon moved, or the turbulent grey eyes when they met his, but he understood he was friend not foe. He was wearing a disguise which made him a hympe? Maybe.

"I'm Donovan," the big guy said, kneeling to place his hands under Obadiah's arms. "This is going to hurt."

No shit.

Hurt didn't even cover it. Pain lanced through Obadiah's body, turning him into a wounded animal. He planted his feet firmly on the ground, saying goodbye to the last of his dignity, and turning to face his new friend. The tight lines of Donovan's face sent a chill down his spine. "You're an empath?" he stuttered, tensing. Definitely a hympe.

Donovan nodded. "I can't block my gift completely." His mouth tilted in a half-smile. "But don't worry, I can't see into your head."

There was a long, tense silence. This stranger had come to his aid, knowing the personal consequences could be brutal. What did you even say to that?

"You okay?" Donovan asked, his voice deeper, gruffer.

"We'll settle for alive. That's about the best I can do right now."

This time the smile reached Donovan's grey eyes. "Then let's get moving."

Draco turned to glare at them, his eyes narrowed on Donovan. He took a step forward, but was hit in the shoulder with a dagger. Draco flicked the knife away as though it was nothing more than an insect, but it was enough to distract him. He shot a ball of energy at Maddison, who dove out of its path. She hit the ground with an 'oof', though she didn't so much as pause to catch her breath.

As Donovan pulled him into the shadows, Obadiah saw her roll once, before flipping to her feet. There was another dagger in her hand.

"This way."

Donovan dragged Obadiah with him, pushing through a door painted the same dull colour as the brick. They entered a room which smelled of stale sweat and motor oil. Pale light filtered through the large glass window at the front, highlighting the grease and grime of an office.

Obadiah leaned on the side of a cluttered desk, trying to catch his breath. Donovan's arms slipped from around his shoulders, and Obadiah almost toppled off the edge in his weakened state.

"What do-"

He broke off when he realised Donovan was no longer beside him. He stared, dumbfounded at the tall, metal filing cabinet against the wall. It blended with the surroundings beautifully, but it hadn't been there a second ago.

Donovan?

As if the hympe could hear his thoughts, or maybe because he thought Obadiah needed confirmation, the doors of the cabinet swung open.

Something powerful hit the door behind him. It was all the incentive Obadiah needed. He hobbled to the cabinet and slumped down on the base. The doors swung shut behind him, plunging him in darkness.

Obadiah waited, ignoring the pain wracking his body as his wounds began to heal. He was regaining some of his strength, and could feel the hum of his power as it began to take root.

Another blast hit the door, and this time Obadiah heard wood splintering. It was disorientating, being able to hear the sound of footsteps in the room and yet blind to the threat. What little powers he'd developed he wanted to save, and focus them on the healing process. So he resisted the urge to reach out with his senses to determine who was in the room with them.

The footsteps receded after a few minutes, only to return again. This time there were more. Obadiah held his breath, half expecting the doors to swing open and reveal his hiding place. To distract himself, he concentrated on the energy humming around him. It was the hympe; he could feel Donovan's apprehension.

It was hard to know how much time passed as he waited patiently in the dark; the minutes began to blend together. Hiding went against all his instincts. Even without his power he wasn't a coward. The only thing that stopped him from facing the threat and playing the odds was his mission. That and the fact Maddison and Donovan had put their lives on the line for him.

Eventually, the doors swung open again, revealing an empty room. Obadiah slipped out, pleased that he could stand unaided. He felt a gentle shift in the air and turned to look at Donovan in his true form. He had the finely sculptured features associated with his kind, one could even call him pretty. The dark brown hair was in bad need of a cut, but Donovan was in good shape. Perhaps he was a hunter.

"Thanks for the assist," Obadiah said, glancing toward the gaping hole in the wall. "What happened to Maddison?"

Donovan's head tilted to the side, his eyes narrowed in suspicion. "How do you know her?"

"Long story. I'll fill you in after we get out of here."

Silence stretch between them as Donovan weighed him up. "Okay. Follow me."

Donovan led him through the front, out onto the road and down another side street. They made it a hundred yards before they ran into Maddison, and she had company. Four demons circled her, their grotesque features lit by a beam of light coming from her braid. Obadiah recognised the species, but couldn't pinpoint a name. His memories were incomplete. Pushing the thought aside, he concentrated on Maddison. Her hair had a life of its own; suspended in the air to her left, rotating in what he could only describe as a taunt.

"Stop playing with them, Maddy," Donovan said. "We need to go."

She laughed, but didn't turn, which was a good thing because the demons moved in unison.

Obadiah watched the elegant dance in front of him, searching his brain for the missing pieces. They didn't come. From his room in the tower, Obadiah had watched the world; monitoring progress within the mortal realm. He decided he hadn't watched Maddison enough.

Her training was evident in the way she anticipated her attackers. Her braid struck the demon closest to her with enough power to lift him off his feet. But Maddison did not rely on her hair alone, she had a blade in each hand, weapons which moved so fast they were but a blur of motion.

It took less than five minutes, while all he could hear was the clashing of metal and the sickening crunch of bone, and four became one.

"Witch!" The curse lost its effect the moment the demon began to whimper like a cornered dog.

"Is that meant to be insulting?" she crooned, and Obadiah shivered against the sound.

He watched her braid wind itself around the demon's neck.

"You're going to tell me your secrets." Maddison laid a hand against his forehead, chanting softly.

The hair dropped away, and Obadiah realised she had bound the demon with gold.

"Congratulations, scumbag. You just won an all-expenses paid trip to the abyss." The moment Maddison released him, he disappeared.

When she turned in his direction, Obadiah was caught by her strong, confident gaze. Her eyes were as green as the Enchanted Forest, and just as lethal. "We need to go." Her gaze shot to Donovan. "Let's move out."

They emerged on a main thoroughfare a minute later, the road deserted but for a number of parked cars on their right. Obadiah hoped one of them belonged to the deadly duo because he didn't know how much longer he could stand. Every part of his body hurt, including an intense pressure under his skin, like his soul was straining to get out.

Donovan nodded. He walked a few steps further onto the street, eyes darting in both directions before he crouched into a kneeling position. A second later a sleek, black car appeared in his place; the engine purring softly.

"Nice choice," Maddy said, guiding Obadiah forward.

The door opened before they reached it and Obadiah stumbled inside with a low groan. The healing process was accelerating at an alarming rate, which was akin to feeling each blow all over again. No wonder so many of the Fallen went mad during the transition.

To distract himself he turned his attention to the driver's seat and Maddison. "How did you manage to gain the services of a hympe?" It had niggled at him. It was the kind of information he should know.

She was silent for a beat or two, and he couldn't tell what she was thinking. "Let's just say Donovan escaped from a particularly charming breed of Nrikabat."

"And when you say charming, you mean they used him as a whipping post," he said, understanding the reason for her scepticism. She owned his contract. "What did they demand for his release?"

"That's not important." Her tone made it clear he wouldn't get an answer. "Donovan has earned his freedom."

Obadiah could have sworn the car purred at her words, which only piqued his interest further. "May I ask where you're taking me?" He had a feeling he knew.

"To a member of the Fallen. I don't know why you're here, or what happened back there, but…" She turned briefly, meeting his eyes. "It's my duty to protect you." Her voice softened. "You can trust us."

He bowed his head in acknowledgement. "How did you happen to find me? Nobody knew of my arrival."

Maddison frowned, which meant she knew the procedure. The Fallen were always met by a Gatekeeper, and supported through the transition. "Let's just say I was in the right place at the right time, and leave it at that."

She was lying. Something or someone had drawn her to his landing site, which meant Draco had been telling the truth. They had sensed his presence. Obadiah decided it didn't matter. Whatever the reason for Maddison's intervention, he owed her more than she could possibly know.

TWO

Zara paced the receiving room, trying not to stare at the Guardians who were huddled together discussing her case. The darkened windows could barely contain the divine light seeping from the group. It glowed at the centre of each being, potent enough to blind. Their beauty could also induce madness; certainly there were few who could comprehend it.

Zara was immune – mostly. Though she was no longer a Guardian; neither was she mortal. She was a member of the Fallen, and had relinquished some of her power for the privilege. Not that she cared about any of that now. Someone was hurting her brethren, and she would beg if it meant the council would intervene.

Lucas broke away from the group and walked towards her. "Zara, how lovely you look," he said, searching her face.

"And you're positively glowing, Luke," she answered with a small smile. "Why don't we cut to the chase?"

He arched a regal brow, amused by her candour. In the mortal realm, Guardians often chose to wear a mask, hiding their true face from the world. Zara couldn't help wondering why Lucas had chosen a disguise. It was true this form was aesthetically pleasing, and yet it was merely a shadow of his true beauty. He towered above her at six foot five, with a large frame and broad shoulders. His fair hair had a slight wave, curling defiantly over his forehead. But his eyes were a reflection of the Lucas she knew, so blue they defied the very colour itself.

She watched his lips curve at her scrutiny. "Am I pleasing, little one?" A reference to her own human size.

"If I didn't know you any better I'd say you were fishing for compliments," she said, eyes twinkling. "This form pales in comparison to your true self."

Lucas inclined his head. "I miss you, Zara."

They had once served together, before she had fallen. "Then you should stop by more often."

"I'll try." He looked back towards the others, focusing once more on his duties. "We discussed your predicament, and have agreed to intervene." He paused, features softening. "But you must understand this is only the beginning, and the Alliance will not take kindly to further interference. Something bigger is happening here."

She bowed her head in acknowledgement, her eyes grateful for the reprieve. "We wouldn't normally call upon you, but we've lost too many of our people."

Something crossed Lucas' face. It might have been pain, but it was too fleeting to decipher. "The Fractured are lending their power to those ill-equipped to handle such responsibility," he said. "As we've seen, it can be dangerous."

Zara though of her cousin. He was nothing more than an empty shell. "May I ask what action you intend to take?"

"So impatient," Lucas chastised gently. "Let us put your mind at ease."

She accepted the hand he offered, following him freely. The room within the conference hall dropped away, to be replaced, less than a heartbeat later, with the filth and grime of an abandoned building. A young woman was kneeling on the floor, dressed in a ceremonial gown. She did not stir at their unexpected arrival, nor did she acknowledge their presence.

Zara's gaze dropped to the Book of Ignis, a volume which had no place in the mortal realm. She moved toward it instinctively, but Lucas pulled her back with a shake of his head.

"It's a trap," he said, scanning the room. "An illusion." He snapped his fingers and the book vanished.

The woman turned, her serene features dissolving into madness. She was clutching a glass cylinder, the chamber glowing bright with an essence Zara recognised.

"You're too late," the woman cackled, raising the cylinder high in the air.

"No!" Zara tried to break free from Lucas' grasp, but he was too strong. She watched helplessly as the woman slammed the vial into the ground.

Lucas sucked in a long breath, mouth wide, chest expanding, as he drew her cousin's energy into his body. When she met his eyes she saw the triumph and felt her heart settle.

A frustrated scream pierced the calm, startling Zara. She turned to see the woman tearing towards them with murder in her eyes. This time when she tugged his hand, Lucas released her. Zara intercepted the woman, slowing her momentum with the flick of a wrist until she slumped into Zara's arms, dazed and confused.

She utilised her empathic gifts and extinguished the fear in the woman's soul. It was only a temporary reprieve because she was too broken; her mind a shadow of its former self. The Fractured viewed her life as expendable, as nothing more than a means to an end.

Laying the woman gently on the ground, Zara looked back at Lucas. "This was too easy, wasn't it?"

"Yes. I don't think Joseph is the target."

Zara shuddered. "They didn't account for the intervention." She bowed her head. "We are in your debt."

"Your family has served us well." He raised his hand, palm toward her. "Give my best to Sebastian," he said, pausing briefly when their fingers connected. "Be well, Zara."

"Stay cool, Luke." She was looking at empty space by the time she felt his palm slip from hers.

Zara turned when she felt the presence of others in the room. The cavalry had arrived to assist the young woman - three members of the same coven. They didn't see her, nor did they see the Guardians who stood watch over them. With a nod of acknowledgement, she bent to touch her fingers to the woman's temple before she transported herself home.

Sebastian was waiting for her; pacing her apartment in a pattern so familiar it made her smile. "Well?" he asked.

"Luke sends his best." She moved to pour herself a drink from the mini-bar. "Joseph is safe."

She caught her brother's smile before he vanished. When he reappeared ten minutes later, Zara had her feet up, sipping from a glass of wine. His grin mirrored the one he'd left with – a merging of past and present in her living space.

"How is Cousin Joseph?"

Sebastian went back to his pacing. "He'll heal. At least he's free."

She noticed a wrinkle on his brow, the after effects of healing. "Sit for a while, Seb. You look tired."

He made a derisive sound in his throat, but sat anyway, hooking a casual arm around her shoulders. "I can't stay long. I'm needed elsewhere."

She could hear the fatigue in his voice, understood the new assignment was taking its toll. "It's a tough one, huh?"

"It would be hell for you."

Zara laid her head against his shoulder. "You feel more than you like to admit."

"All I feel right now is anger. The Fractured don't have the monopoly on pain. There's darkness in all of us, and I witness it every day."

"Then the humans are right and we're all demons," she murmured, weighed down by the burden of her brother's sorrow. "A war is coming, Sebastian, and it will be worse than anything we've seen."

As she spoke, she opened herself up to him, sneaking past his defences to take away the hurt. For once he didn't protest. "How many have you lost?" she whispered.

"Thirty-eight." He sighed, a sign of weakness he allowed only because it was her. "Even with all we know, the steps we take to ease the transition, it's hard when we lose them." He shifted, uncomfortable with his thoughts. "Luke is around, and that helps."

The fall had been hard on Sebastian and Lucas. They were partners in crime, friends, and though that would never change, they were on different paths now. It was a natural progression for Sebastian. As Guardian, it was his duty and privilege to guide souls through the transition, so when he fell, those abilities extended to other members of the Fallen. Sebastian helped his comrades adapt to their new home and, when the time came, he supported souls leaving this life and going on to the next.

"And what of Zachariah?" she asked, surprised he wasn't glued to her brother's side.

They each had a Charge, assigned as protector by the Legion of Watchers. Zachariah was a vampire, one whose service, whose protection of the mortal realm, had earned him the right to watch over Sebastian.

"Zac has problems of his own, but he's around," he said, in a tone that told her to butt out.

She let it go. For now. "I'm worried, Seb. It's clear the Guardians are, too, and they wouldn't tell me how the Fractured are binding our kind." In truth, she hadn't thought it possible. They were former Guardians, and nobody had the power to control them. Or so she thought.

Sebastian leant forward to kiss her temple. "We'll figure it out, sis. And I'll ask around." He sat up. "But I have to go. Thanks for representing us at the meeting."

The hand she was squeezing to express her affection evaporated. She stared at the empty space and felt doubt niggle at her. In reducing or extracting pain, her brother ultimately paid the price. She'd learned that the hard way.

Her gift at detecting emotions was also part curse. She could reflect and manipulate the energies around her; good or bad. Finding ways to protect herself didn't make it any easier. With each passing year the hole inside her widened, an inexplicable emptiness she had never been able to explain. It was a constant ache now.

Brushing it aside, she settled back against the pillows. *'Goodnight, brother,'* she said, knowing the echo in her mind would reach him.

'Be well, Zar.' The whisper, followed by a faint laugh, made her smile. Her family were safe, and she intended to keep it that way.

***

By the time they reached their destination, Obadiah's powers were practically restored. He could have removed the flimsy barrier in front of him, but he found himself waiting patiently for the door to open.

Maddison tapped her foot, as impatient as he, though he felt no need to expel the useless energy. The itch beneath his skin was growing stronger, and with it the tether of control was wearing thin.

He felt her before she opened the door, and he wasn't prepared for the onslaught of emotion. He had to lock it down tight. Zara was small, though her petite form did nothing to mask her potency. Her pale gold hair hung in a curtain around her face, a stark contrast against her rich mahogany eyes. Those eyes were pinning him to the ground, suspicion and just a touch of concern clouding their glorious shade.

They flicked to Maddison and narrowed like laser beams. "What's going on?" she demanded.

"I was hoping you could tell me," Maddison said, stepping forward. "He's one of you guys, obviously."

Zara turned back to him and he felt her power push against his defences. "No. He's not."

Obadiah didn't know whether to be amused or angry when Maddison whipped out a dagger.

"I don't understand. He smells like a Fallen."

He settled on humour, enjoying the sound as it erupted from his throat. "I'll take that as a compliment."

Zara's eyes darted down the hall before settling on him again. It took her a moment, a moment in which he knew she was determining the threat. "Let's take this inside."

She rounded on him before the door was fully closed. "Who are you?" It was a demand.

Maddison, he noticed, had positioned herself between them. Interesting.

"I'm here to help," he answered, not yet ready to reveal himself.

"And I'm going to need more than that." She turned to Maddison and placed a hand on her arm. "Watch him." A second later she was gone, and he felt the loss far too quickly.

"What the hell is going on?" Maddison asked, taking a step towards him.

He allowed the show of dominance because he wanted answers too, and she wasn't going to evade this time. "How did you know of my arrival?" he asked, watching her.

"I didn't." Maddison tilted her head to the side. "I was drawn to the city."

This time, he took the step until they were mere inches apart. Her eyes widened when she detected his power, but not in fear. "What kind of witch are you?"

She seemed to consider the question, and he couldn't be sure whether or not she would have answered. Zara's return settled it. Maddison stepped away from him, resuming her defensive stance. The message was clear.

A few seconds later, Lucas appeared. "Obadiah," he said, bowing elegantly.

"Holy shit, who is this guy?" Maddison asked, looking from him to Lucas and back again.

"I know it's hard, chosen one, but you should show a little respect," Lucas chastised, and Obadiah's curiosity hitched up another level. "We're in the presence of a Prime."

"One of the Seven?" Zara spluttered, paling at the unexpected news.

"I'm guessing that's important."

Obadiah laughed, amused by Maddison. He was anxious to delve into her history. "Strictly speaking I'm working alone," he said, turning his attention to Zara. "I fell because you're in danger, and-"

"You fell?" Lucas said, horrified. "But how? Why?"

"He's not permitted to exist in this realm in any other way," Zara answered for him. "Why would you risk expulsion for me?"

Obadiah could feel her mind buffering against his as she tried to search for answers. It was like a caress, threatening to weaken his resolve. He was tempted to let her in, to allow her to see the truth.

"Because I didn't have a choice." He knew he was on dangerous ground. The less they all knew, the better. At least until he discovered who they could trust. Not even Obadiah's closest allies knew he intended to fall. Yet, somehow, Draco had found out.

"What can I do?" Lucas asked.

"Deny all knowledge of this conversation until you're summoned. I need time. That's all I ask."

Lucas turned to Zara, his conflict clear. But the implied danger to her safety was enough to sway his decision. With a nod, he disappeared without another word.

"What's the threat and how do we stop it?" Maddison asked, walking to stand beside Zara. "Does it have anything to do with the Band of Ubiquity?"

You continue to surprise me, witch.

"How do you know about that?" In truth, it made his job easier. He had broken too many rules already, and this saved him from adding a ring to the noose. Volunteering the information would be viewed as an unfair advantage by the council. Confirming it, on the other hand, was an acceptable compromise.

"It was the only thing inside the Sentinel demon's head, probably because it was his most closely guarded secret." Maddison grinned. "He was trying so hard to keep the information from me he was practically screaming it."

Obadiah's mind flashed to the demon she had sent into the abyss. He almost felt sorry for him. Almost.

"If they're making a move to steal the Fae Queen's bracelet, then we're in more trouble than I thought," Zara said, paling.

Maddison frowned. "Back up a minute. What does Draco and his minions want with a piece of jewellery?"

"A piece of jewellery?" Zara laughed, a musical sound he hadn't heard in hundreds of years. "That jewellery will enable Draco to access whatever realm he chooses, which includes an unrestricted pass into Empyrean itself."

Maddison's expression was priceless. Obadiah had to bite down on his lip to prevent a laugh.

"And they let her walk around with that thing?"

"Two things," Obadiah said, cutting to the chase. "Nobody *lets* Aretha do anything, and few have access to her realm without her expressed permission. Also, Ubiquity doesn't work in isolation. It's simply a key, one which will take Draco one step further to achieving his ultimate goal."

"Okay, that makes more sense than using all that power as a fashion accessory." Maddison grinned when Zara tugged on her braid. The rings in her hair were not simply adornments; Maddison used them to focus her magic. "Point well made." She dipped her head before turning back to Obadiah. "But what does all that have to do with the Fallen?"

He took a second to consider his options as two pairs of eyes turned in his direction; neither woman would let the subject drop. It meant he had to give them something. "Only Guardians can enter Aretha's kingdom uninvited, and as descendants, he plans to build a Fallen army."

Zara's eyes grew huge. "That's why they're binding us. Do you know how?" she asked.

"They need the blood of a Guardian." Obadiah regretted the words as soon as they formed. He'd already said too much. "That's all I'm permitted to tell you right now." He looked down at himself and winced. "I could use a fresh pair of clothes. Perhaps you would permit me to get cleaned up before we continue this discussion."

At full power he could have negated such need, but found he was glad for the breathing space. Zara was still pushing against his barriers, trying to get a read on him. His control had never held up where she was concerned.

She gazed down at his torn and bloodied clothes. "Of course." Zara moved toward a hallway on their right. "I have some of my brother's clothes in the guest room. You can use those."

As he followed, Obadiah heard the distinct sound of a phone at his back. Maddison cursed a second later, but he didn't turn. Nor did Zara.

"I'll be right back," Maddison called out.

Zara stopped at the first door and glanced back. She met his eyes briefly before looking over his shoulder. "I suppose it's useless to remind you it's your night off?"

"In this job, there's no such thing," came the hurried reply, followed by the sound of the door closing.

"She's an interesting choice for a Watcher," Obadiah commented to fill the silence.

"Maddy is a lot of things, and interesting is certainly one of them."

Obadiah heard the almost defensive tone to her voice. It surprised him. "You've become attached."

Zara laughed as she opened the door to the guest room. "She's a keeper." She stepped aside to allow him to enter, her curiosity obvious. "I'll make you something to eat while you freshen up. One thing I remember from my own transition; falling works up quite an appetite."

He didn't get a chance to respond, and was glad of it. The close proximity was draining him, which meant he wasn't as strong as he thought. When it came to Zara he doubted he ever would be. He'd risked his life and his standing in order to protect her, but never expected to lose his sanity. If he didn't mend his barriers, she would learn too much, too quickly.

THREE

Maddison jogged down the apartment steps two at a time as she listened to Riley on the other end of the phone. As fellow hunters, they often relied on each other. Riley was calling in a favour.

"I could really use your expertise on this one," he said, sounding pissed about his current assignment. "A newly formed coven, with a lame ass name, made a deal with a Sentinel demon and it backfired."

"They seem to be getting around." She thought of her own run-in.

"What?"

"Never mind." She pushed through the exit and out into the night. "How lame are we talking?"

"Sisters of Darkness. It's like they're asking for trouble." His growl was loud enough to travel to Donovan, who was waiting for her on the steps. "Are you going to help or not?"

"I'm a little tied up at the moment."

Riley grunted. "Business or pleasure?"

She laughed as she dropped down next to Donovan. "I'll catch you up later. The best thing I can do right now is send Donovan to cover for me."

There was a moment of silence on the other end. "What does Tempest have to say about that?"

Maddy rolled her eyes at the nickname. "He says he'll see you in twenty. Later."

She snapped the phone shut and met those stormy grey eyes, which had earned Donovan the title. "Have you given any thought to what you'll do when the contract is up?"

The heat of his anger burned, more because he couldn't deny her the request. Not if she demanded it. "Telling you to go to hell is first on the list," he said, turning away. "How can I watch your back if you send me on a dummy assignment?"

"There's a Sentinel demon on the loose, does that sound like I'm joking around to you?" She knew what he meant. Riley could handle the aftermath, with or without them. But the fact remained he had a better chance with Donovan at his side. "I know you enjoy training with him, so why not put those skills to good use in the field?"

"I train so I'm better able to protect you. I have no interest in fighting the good fight, as Riley likes to put it."

Maddy narrowed her eyes at him. "That's bullshit, and you know it. It's not your job to protect me, Donovan. And I have a partner."

He burst to his feet, rounding on her before she could blink. "Oh that's right. You keep me around because you feel sorry for me."

Maddy was on her feet and in his face a heartbeat later. "Don't take it out on me because you're afraid to live. You're free, Donovan. You should be happy about that."

The silence whipped around them, alive with the tension which had been brewing for weeks.

"Did it ever occur to you I might choose *this* life? I'm not afraid to live. The point is I want to for the first time in my miserable existence." He turned to jog down the steps. "I thought you understood that."

What the hell?

She watched him disappear into the shadows, heading for the portal a hundred yards on the right. Thanks to a sorcerer with a sense of humour, almost every street sign was a gateway to a different destination.

"Well, shit," she muttered, dropping back down. "That went well."

The first few weeks after winning Donovan's contract she had had no idea what to do with him; didn't particularly want the responsibility. But they had a connection she couldn't deny, and so she'd encouraged his interest in her work. Donovan made an excellent partner in crime, and there were days she didn't know how she coped without him.

Yet, despite the friendship which had grown between them, she'd never expected him to stay. To want to stay. He deserved his own life, and she didn't want him clinging to some misguided notion he owed her. She didn't want that. Didn't want him to feel duty-bound to her. It didn't mean she wanted him to disappear. Over the last few months she had begun to hope he would accept Tobias' offer to join the League.

Maddison rubbed her hands over her face. She was fooling herself, because his sense of duty wasn't the only thing that frightened her. She was terrified of letting him down, of not living up to his expectations. Donovan's past was shadowed in darkness, and, despite his forgiving nature, he trusted no one. No one but her and, in most respects, Riley. How could she not fail, given her history? It shamed her. Was she so hardened she couldn't allow him to need her, to rely on her?

'Hey...kid.'

The affectionate term, which usually amused Donovan because he was much older, was met by silence. Her mind was empty.

'Just stay safe, okay.'

Still nothing. She could have demanded a response, but in doing so it would damage the trust between them.

"Great. Just great." She said, aloud this time, as she jumped to her feet and turned back to the apartment.

She didn't have time to dwell on her own problems, because Zara was shit deep in her own. If what the Prime said was true, things were about to get ugly. Fast. The Fractured were always making waves, they excelled at it. But they hadn't made a major move against the Alliance since the Demonic War, and she had no doubt they had a solid plan to bring down the heavens.

When she let herself into the apartment, Zara was on the couch with her feet propped up and a glass of wine in her hand, a suspiciously large glass. Of course, the moment their eyes met, concern flooded Zara's face. Clearly, Maddison hadn't done a good enough job closing down her emotions.

Zara patted the seat beside her, a little too forcefully. "Sit, and tell me what's wrong."

Her lips twitched, despite the command. She might be Zara's Watcher, but they were also friends, and Maddison had never been able to hide anything from her.

She plucked the wine glass from Zara's hand and took a long swallow before handing it back with a grin. "It's my night off. Remember?"

A second glass of wine appeared in Zara's hand. "Knock yourself out." Her eyes narrowed. "But while you're drinking yourself into a stupor, you can tell me what's bothering you."

Maddy stared at the grape red liquid for a minute. "I sent Donovan to help Riley with a job and he resents me for it."

"Donovan or Riley?"

"He thinks I need protection," Maddy said, ignoring the question.

Zara took a sip of wine, regarding her over the rim. "You're the first person who cared whether he lived or died. That's a sad but sorry truth. As far as Donovan sees it, you're his…family. His to protect. I thought you understood that."

Maddison closed her eyes on a long, slow groan. "Why do you have to be so damn reasonable? I feel like a total bitch."

"Give him time. He knows you're just looking out for him."

She shook her head, downing the glass without taking a breath. Zara merely smiled at her discomfort.

"How do you do that? I haven't even told you what I said."

"I know you, and so does Donovan. Yes, you can be a bitch. But we both love you anyway."

Maddy's surprised laugh echoed around them. She sat back against the cushions, feeling too relaxed. Zara's power didn't work on her, so it wasn't her friend's feel-good vibe. It was most definitely the alcohol.

Smart move, Maddy.

She was lucky they had an angel on their side and were safely tucked away in Zara's apartment. Heavens forbid she actually had to fight her way out of the drunken haze. Speaking of which.

"What did you do to deserve the attention of that particular angel?" Maddison asked, turning her head in Zara's direction.

"I have absolutely no idea." Zara glanced towards the hall. "I don't know whether to be flattered or terrified by the intervention."

Maddison couldn't fault her for that. "Did you get a read on him?"

"No." Zara frowned. "It's like he feels nothing."

"He's a tough cookie all right. His welcoming committee really went to town on him and he barely made a sound."

"How did they detect his arrival if we didn't?" Zara wondered aloud.

"Beats me. It's like I was drawn there."

Zara laughed at the innocent expression. "Trouble has a way of finding you."

"Hey," she said, pouting a little. "I saved hot stuff in there. I should get credit for that."

"And brought trouble to my door."

"Yeah, but he's a nice kind of trouble." Maddison wiggled her eyebrows. "You should take advantage of that while he's here."

Zara blushed, clearly the thought had occurred to her. "You don't hit on a Prime."

"I'm struggling to picture you hitting on anybody." Maddison laughed when the blush deepened, turning the colour of the wine in Zara's glass.

She was saved further embarrassment when Sebastian appeared before them, with Zachariah in tow.

The first thing Maddison noticed was the weary expression on Zachariah's face. She'd long since seen past the classic beauty that turned most of the population into a puddle of lust at his feet. By his very nature he drew people in. He was well over 6ft with a lithe, toned body, and dark, flawless skin. His eyes were a forbidden chocolate, and haunted. It sent a prickle of apprehension along her skin. Her brother was hurting.

"I take it you spoke to Lucas," Zara said, glancing at Sebastian.

"Yes, I came to make sure you're okay."

Maddison jumped to her feet and jammed her hands on her hips. "That's why I'm here, pretty boy."

The name usually irritated Sebastian, but for once he let it go. She narrowed her eyes at him, assessing whether his reticence had anything to do with Zachariah. Sebastian was nothing like his sister; in looks or temperament. The vessel they took when they fell was the reason for this lack of family resemblance. Sebastian's hair was a darker blonde, his eyes an intense blue.

"Do we know the purpose of his visit?" Sebastian asked, getting straight to the point.

Maddison decided she hadn't finished tormenting him, so she jumped in before Zara could. "He's on vacation. Apparently the Enchanted Realm is nice this time of year." When Sebastian still didn't raise to the bait, Maddison shrugged and walked around the table to punch Zachariah on the arm. Her usual greeting. "Hey, bloodsucker," she said lightly.

"Hag," he responded with a toothy grin.

"He was about to tell us how the Fractured are binding members of the Fallen, but he had to go to the powder room," Maddison said, after a small silence.

Sebastian smirked. "You know a Prime has the power to smite you where you stand, even in this realm."

"And yet the Prime is oddly amused by her," Obadiah said, walking down the hall.

Maddison glanced at Zara guiltily, who was lit up like a red neon sign. The angel had hearing like a bat, so he'd no doubt caught their earlier exchange.

Note to self. Learn to keep your mouth shut.

She turned as Sebastian bowed his head in greeting. "If I'd known of your arrival, I would have-"

Obadiah raised a hand, cutting him off. "Nobody knew of my intention to fall, so don't take it personally."

"And you believe my sister's life is in danger?" Sebastian asked, unfazed.

"Yes."

"I've been thinking about what you said, about using the blood of a Guardian to bind us," Zara said, capturing their attention. "Are we to assume the rumours are true? That those who are disgraced and stripped of their rank are sent to the mortal realm?"

Maddison frowned, thinking it over. If that were the case, the angels Zara spoke of would be human; born of mortal parents and destined to live out their existence on Earth. It made sense; binding spells normally required blood, and the essence of a Fallen was not part of the vessel's DNA. But it didn't explain how the Fractured were gaining control. Not fully.

"If Draco is draining a disgraced Guardian of their blood, how is he using it to bind the Fallen?" she asked, ignoring Sebastian's disapproving stare. If he had his way she would be out of sight and out of mind. A protector of old.

Obadiah stared at her, so long and hard she thought he might smite her after all.

Seriously? Who still uses the word smite?

"You're the witch," Obadiah said. "Why don't you tell us?"

She picked up the gauntlet, pacing in a tight circle as her mind flicked through the options. "It has to be a powerful spell. And he would need a sorcerer, or a strong coven to perform the tethering ritual."

There were those who bound demons and other species; stealing their soul and tapping into their power. An image of Tobias Locke, the Hympe King popped into her head. She had saved him from such a fate only the year before. The Fractured seemed hell bent on creating a specialised army. It was no surprise they were stealing souls to do it.

"The only possible way is for the Guardian's blood to come into contact with the target." Maddison glanced at Zara. "Was Joseph attacked prior to the separation?" It was how other species described the experience; their very essence ripped from their body until they were an empty shell.

"How are you so sure you're right?" Sebastian asked, and she swore she heard a note of respect in his voice.

Maddison glanced at Zachariah, unsurprised he was being the good soldier and blending into the background. "Because it's the only explanation that makes sense, and angel-boy didn't correct me."

"I think I might go ahead with the smiting after all," Obadiah said, turning to Zara. "You won't miss her too much I take it?"

Zara shrugged. "A slight inconvenience at best."

"Seriously? You could choke up a little remorse, at least," Maddison said, but she was laughing. It seemed Mr Big Shot had a sense of humour.

"I'll spare your life," Obadiah told her, his face solemn. She didn't buy it, especially as his eyes were lit with mischief. "But you will not refer to me as angel-boy."

"Yes, sir, Your Primeness." She grinned at the sound of Sebastian's groan. "But seriously, how does Zara fit into Draco's scheme?"

The light went out of Obadiah's eyes so quickly, they appeared inky black in their intensity. "The main reason is her empathic ability. If they use her to lead the army, she can manipulate Aretha's forces into doing her bidding. At least long enough for reinforcements to break through."

Something about his answer didn't ring true. She had no doubt it was one of the reasons. It just wasn't the main one. "So what's your plan? I take it you have one."

"We have to get a message to Aretha, and warn her of what's coming."

Sebastian moved to sit beside Zara. He put his hand in hers in a gentle show of solidarity. "There's one thing I don't understand," he said, his eyes on Obadiah. "If you knew about their plan, then the Alliance know, so why aren't they intervening?"

Points to Seb.

Maddison watched Obadiah carefully. She didn't have Zara's ability to read his emotional state, but it didn't take a genius to know he was hiding something.

"Because they can't interfere directly, not until the Fractured threaten the mortal realm in some way."

"What makes you so different? Just how many rules are you willing to break?" Zachariah asked.

Obadiah sighed and shoved a hand through his hair. "It's the reason I fell. To create a more even playing field. My powers are considerably less when confined in this way." He looked away, clearly unhappy with the direction of the conversation. "But you're right. It's a fine line between arming you fairly, and giving too much of an advantage"

Sebastian stood again, and walked to stand beside Zachariah. "Warning Aretha seems like our best option. How soon do you need to leave?"

"My arrival is not the secret I was hoping for," Obadiah said. "I guess you could say time is of the essence."

In the silence that followed, Maddison locked eyes with Zachariah. *'Come find me when you're free. We need to talk,'* she said through their link. He nodded once, head bowed when Sebastian put a hand on his shoulder.

"I need to juggle a few things," Sebastian said, his words echoing in the empty space when he transported out with Zachariah.

"Why don't I make us a snack?" Maddison suggested, glancing at Zara. "Oh, come on Zar, don't look at me like that. I need to contact Tobias if we're taking a trip into the Enchanted Realm, and to do that, I have to do something productive with my hands or I might break something!"

"You have a direct link to the Hympe King?" Obadiah asked, cutting through Zara's laugh.

Maddison wrinkled her nose. "It's a long story, but yes. We shared a blood bond and now he's in my head more often than not. I'd prefer to speak to him face to face." She paused to give him a pointed look. "But time is of the essence."

"What is it?" Zara asked, watching Obadiah's expression.

"I'm not sure. My memories should have returned, but there are gaps I can't fathom." He waved the thought away. "I know everything I need to right now."

"Well, okay then," Maddison said, winking at Zara. "I'll let you two catch up." She walked out into the hall, headed for the kitchen.

FOUR

Maddison sliced the skin from a pineapple in clean, smooth strokes. She was working on auto pilot, oblivious to the mountain of fruit she had already cut, as she waited for Tobias to answer her telepathic hail.

'I heard about your handiwork in the capital.' Came the distinctively arrogant response in her head. *'Please tell me you don't need me to bail you out.'*

'Like that's ever going to happen.' It annoyed her that she'd missed him. She hadn't seen him in weeks, and even his virtual presence had been lacking. His pause annoyed her even more, there was a smugness to his silence.

'I know you don't want to gloat, which leaves the obvious and my favourite choice, that you miss me.'

'You got me. I'm hacking away at a perfectly good piece of fruit because I can't live without your dulcet tones in my head for another second.' This time his silence made her smile. *'What do you know about Primes?'* she added, while she had the advantage.

'Highest order of angels, seven in total, and commanders of the Battalion.'

She was more familiar with the Battalion. During the war she had worked alongside a number of warrior angels. *'Have you ever known one to fall?'* More silence, but this time she didn't know how to feel about it.

'So that's what all the chatter is about. There's a Prime in the mortal realm.'

'His name is Obadiah, and Donovan and I interrupted his welcome to earth party.' She let that hang, slightly disappointed when there was no comeback. *'He needs access to Aretha's realm, which means a clear path through the Enchanted Forest.'*

'And you want my help? What makes you think I want to put myself in the line of fire?'

'Come on, Tobias. If you want me to ask nicely, you can at least try to be more convincing. This is exactly the kind of assignment you enjoy.' The Enchanted League were renowned for their protection detail, and since Tobias was the founder, with a particular axe to grind against the Fractured, it was his dream job.

'We have our hands full at the moment, so it depends how nice you're willing to be.'

It was a relief to hear his amusement. That she could handle. *'How about I don't kick your ass for pushing the advantage?'*

Laugher filled her head, and she realised she'd missed that too. *'I can handle a little one on one. Some would say I need the exercise.'*

'Then I'll look forward to it.' She glanced down at the chunks of fruit, all laid out in neat little rows. *'It's happening soon, so anyone you can spare I'd appreciate it.'*

'I'll get a team ready, or I will as soon as you say the magic words.' More of the laughter. *'You can do it, Maddy. It's for a good cause.'*

She opened a cupboard and pulled out a box of skewers. Taking her time, she began to load up the fruit. When she could stand the silence no longer, she let the grin into her mental voice. *'I've missed you, half-blood.'*

'I know it, witch.'

Maddison rolled her eyes, aware he would anticipate the gesture and not expect a response. She was just loading the snacks onto a tray when Zara walked into the kitchen.

"I take it from the smile things went well," she said, glancing at Maddison's handiwork.

"We have assistance from the League," Maddison confirmed, handing over the goods. "But I don't think we should rush in blindly, Zar."

They were both silent as they returned to the living room. To fill the tension, Maddison snagged a skewer and bit into fresh pineapple, letting the juice zing across her tongue.

Obadiah was watching them curiously. He gave Zara a quizzical look when she placed the tray in front of him.

"Maddy and I have been working on her anger issues, and this is the side benefit." Zara smiled innocently. "Help yourself."

He did just that, waving his skewer towards Maddison in silent acknowledgement. "Did the Hympe King agree to assist?"

Maddison had to bite her tongue before she answered. So much for her anger management. "Tobias is gathering a team," she answered, with only the slightest emphasis on his name. The pause helped. "He's good to go when you are."

"Then we go at first light."

"You need to settle a few things of your own," Zara said, with a pointed look at Maddison. "Go. We'll be fine until you get back."

She thought about it for perhaps a millisecond. She needed a change of clothes, her favourite weapons, and the chance to catch up with Donovan. "Okay. But if you need me-"

"I'll call. I promise."

Maddison nodded once, turning towards the door before she could change her mind and decide to stay put. She felt no threat from Obadiah, so she had no doubt Zara was safe. Yet, he was hiding something, something important. Judging by all the energy vibrating in the air, it had something to do with Zara, and she was going to find out exactly what it was. Even if she had to do something repulsive, like call on Orion Reece.

***

Obadiah felt Zara pushing against his barriers, her curiosity reaching out like a touch. It was so familiar it made his heart ache.

"What is it?" she asked, and he wondered if he'd let his guard slip. "You've been on edge since we spoke of Tobias. Is he in danger too?"

I'm on edge because of you.

He shook his head. "I don't think so. But there's a gap in my memory, and it has something to do with your witch."

She turned in her seat. "Whatever it is, you can count on her. We need her on our side."

"What can you tell me about Donovan?" he asked, shifting to mirror her position. "I find the relationship he shares with Maddison…unique."

"You could say that." Zara smiled, her eyes dreamy as though she were remembering something. "Donovan shares a similar empathic ability, and I've taught him how to control the gift. He's one of the gentlest creatures I know, and his strength is truly admirable." She paused, looking down at her hands. "Maddy doesn't know how to deal with their connection. It's like nothing I've seen outside of a familial bond."

"And what of her connection to Tobias?"

Now she laughed. "You'll have to figure that one out for yourself. I wouldn't even know where to begin."

It had been so long since he heard her laugh he felt momentarily stunned. The silence grew between them, a thick, tense cloud which, in itself, was familiar.

"Why do I get the feeling we've met before?" she asked, watching his face.

He stood, feeling uncomfortable in his own skin. Except it wasn't his own; this body was merely a vessel. "There are things I'm forbidden to share, and that's one of them."

"Are you saying my memories were-" The words fell away when Sebastian returned with Zachariah. It annoyed Obadiah that he gave no warning; though he could hardly knock on air.

His mind tuned out as Sebastian began to update Zara on his plans. It gave him time to repair his shields. Wandering over to the small bar in the far corner of the room, he studied the small ornaments lined up along a glass shelf.

Obadiah had watched Zara for years, telling himself it was a matter of ensuring her safety. How foolish. How naive for someone with his power. Zara was the reason he tortured himself. The reason he followed her movements, blind to everything but her. The apartment, the details he missed; it was proof of his obsession. But then, it had never been any different. Since the day they met, his heart belonged to Zara. How might she feel, he wondered, if he told her the real reason he had fallen. For her, and her alone. It hardly mattered they could never be together; a life without her, without the inherent light which shone from her very core. Obadiah would cease to exist.

She'd kick you the hell out, that's what.

Zara's memories no longer included him. Their time together had been stolen from them both. The only difference was, he remembered everything. He had to live an eternity with his mistakes. The burden was his. It would remain that way.

Obadiah spun on his heels at the sound of Zara's muffled groan. She was doubled over in pain, clutching her chest. He was by her side with merely a thought.

"What is it?" Sebastian asked, concern making his voice hitch.

"Gregory," Zara sobbed out in terror. "Something's happening to Gregory."

A second later Sebastian was gone, taking Zachariah with him.

"Who's Gregory?" Obadiah asked, lifting Zara off her feet in one fluid movement.

"He's my Ward," she said, gritting her teeth against the pain.

"Show me," he whispered, and cupped her cheek with his hand. He felt the connection like a lance through his heart. He knew it was dangerous, that lowering his defences came with a price. But he couldn't stand by and watch her suffer.

He didn't care that she accepted the pain as part of her gift, or that she would be angry with him for the distraction. By forcing her into a memory she would know peace for a while, and he would see what needed to be done.

Obadiah felt a wave of frustration. His powers were not fully operational after all, because he should have been able to access the memories with a mere thought. Instead, he wasted precious time establishing a stronger link between them, making himself vulnerable.

Pushing the thoughts away, he travelled into Zara's mind and allowed her to choose where she took him. An image formed in his head, a fourteen-year old boy leaned against a lamp-post. No, not a boy. It was Zara, using a filter to deflect her true form. She hadn't changed her shape, so when he concentrated on the boy, he could see past the illusion.

After a moment, he settled himself into the memory and, like a movie, the scene sprang to life. Obadiah felt everything as Zara did; the nerves dancing in her belly, exacerbated by the cacophony of emotions coming from the environment. The assignment was important to her, he felt the echo of it, the connection.

Obadiah sensed the presence of Zara's Ward as she did, and took a moment to admire her timing. He took a step back to watch the scene unfold, saw Zara as the teenage boy, head turned away from her Ward, and yet acutely aware of the space around them. There was a shift in the air as the young boy approached, a shift Zara took advantage of - stepping into his path so they collided. Books scattered across the pavement, the thud echoing inside Obadiah's head as he tried to rein in the influx of emotion.

Zara absorbed the anguish emanating from the boy, giving Obadiah a whole new respect for her talents. He found it as distracting as hell, especially the jumbled thoughts she was picking up like a radio antennae.

'I wasn't looking,' 'I'm so stupid,' 'Careless,' the Ward's thoughts punched into her, bruising in their intensity.

"Sorry, I wasn't paying attention." Obadiah heard her say, and her voice held just the right amount of irritation.

"No, it was my fault," the boy mumbled, eyes downcast as he tried to collect the work settling around them.

"Wow, did you clean out your locker? I've never seen so much stuff."

Obadiah caught the hitch in her voice, but the boy obviously didn't.

"I…" Bright colour rose in his cheeks.

"I'm messing with you." When all the books were neatly stacked, Zara stuck out a hand, waiting until the boy looked up before she spoke again. "I'm Jerry. I think we have science together."

Her Ward looked confused as he tried to place Jerry's face.

Zara's appearance was non-threatening, but Obadiah knew how nervous she was about making the right choice. It was as confusing as hell. The bombardment of so many thoughts and feelings, it was wearing his reserves to their limit.

He concentrated on the image he knew the boy could see; a thin body, with bones jutting out in awkward angles. The teenage acne was a nice touch, and her filter's eyes were a clear, crystal blue.

"I'm new here," she said, when the boy continued to stare. "My parents drag me to a new town every six months or so."

That provoked a response. He hooked the books under his arm and stood again. "I have to go. Maybe I'll see you at school."

Obadiah saw it was a lie. The knowledge inside Zara's head told him the boy was planning to take his own life. A sense of hopelessness was leaking out of him like a fine mist. He felt alone, so very alone.

Zara didn't let him off the hook that easily. "Why don't I tag along for a while? I don't have anything better to do."

"Erm…well, I suppose, if you want to." He began walking, his face creased into a mask of confusion.

To Zara, his expression was a beautiful thing. Confusion was good, she could work with that. Indifference would mean it was too late.

"So, have you got a name?" she asked.

"Gregory." He didn't look up, but there was a smile on his face.

"Good to meet you, Gregory. Most people kind of ignore me." She gave a careless shrug. "They think I'm weird."

"I didn't say you weren't weird."

That earned him a laugh. Zara was well aware of Gregory's potential, of the many things he would accomplish if given the chance.

"You got me there."

As they walked towards Gregory's house, Obadiah relaxed into the memory, and allowed Zara to relive the moment they'd made a connection. For some reason, Gregory touched a chord in her, and he was more curious than ever.

They'd spent hours together that day, but the memory was fleeting. He sensed Zara returning to consciousness, her every muscle tense.

"I can't feel him anymore." Her voice was so small and vulnerable it broke his heart.

"I'm sure Sebastian's doing everything he can."

She sat up so quickly they almost bumped heads. "I have to…"

Obadiah knew she was about to transport to her brother's location, because she wasn't thinking clearly. A sense of desperation slithered through him because he couldn't force her to stay, not if he wanted to gain her trust. So he settled for distraction; giving in to a desire of the flesh he didn't fully understand. He kissed her.

If sharing her memories was dangerous, this was suicidal. The physical impact was so unexpected he felt the barrier in his mind crack under the pressure. If she discovered the truth, felt even an ounce of his true feelings, it would be over. But nothing could have prepared him for the feel of her, the taste of her lips. He'd imagined how it would be so many times, the fantasies were often the only thing to stave off his loneliness. His need for her. He understood then, that going home, losing her, would be so much worse than loving her from afar.

The pain of it spread across his chest, and while it hurt, it was nothing compared to the pleasure coursing through him. She gasped and opened up to him, her hands twisting into his shirt. The barrier cracked again, threatened to crumble under the wave of longing. It disturbed him to realise he didn't care, he would have let the chips fall if Zara hadn't pushed against his chest, forcing him to release her.

Her eyes were huge when they focused on him. "What the hell was that?" she demanded.

He wanted to hang his head in shame, especially when he saw the confused arousal in her eyes. He'd behaved like a total ass. "I needed to stop you from leaving," he said, and watched anger ignite her eyes. The fact it made him want to kiss her again somehow made it worse.

When she froze, Obadiah went on instant alert. A second later Sebastian arrived.

"He's fine." Her brother dropped down in front of her and took her hands. "There was an attack at his dorm, but he's unharmed."

"What kind of attack?" Zara searched Sebastian's face.

"Raptures, a team of three. There's a lot of confusion at the university, but Zachariah is dealing with it." Sebastian stroked a hand over her hair. "I wanted to let you know your Ward is safe."

"And what if they return?"

Obadiah resisted the urge to smooth the concern from her face. Raptures were rogue members of the Enraptured, and brutal if used by the wrong hands. They had tremendous healing power, could repair a wounded soul with nothing more than their presence. But when they went dark, the opposite was true. They radiated negative energy in waves. Could tap into even the smallest darkness and exploit it.

"I have protection in place, and we'll be alerted immediately." Sebastian stood. "I don't think they'll resist further exposure, and Gregory is safer where he is. For now."

"Okay." Zara stood, and when she spoke again her voice was stronger. "Okay. You should go. Zachariah can't deal with the aftermath alone."

"It's fortunate your Watcher is a vampire," Obadiah said, his mind still on the creatures.

Zachariah would be altering their memories, easing their confusion after the attack. It seemed apt, especially given that Vampires were also descendants of the Enraptured. They had a positive effect on humans; they had been helping them for millennia.

But why attack Zara's Ward? What did they hope to achieve?

Obadiah glanced up as Sebastian was phasing out. He stared at the empty space he left behind, searching his brain. It hit him like a punch to the gut. He knew exactly who Gregory was, and why he'd been taken.

FIVE

Maddison sat on the stone steps outside Merc Hall, staring into the fountain. The feature sat in the middle of a square, facing the once prominent building. It now housed the mercenaries in the area, freelance hunters who needed a sense of community, even if they couldn't admit it. She'd named their sanctuary Merc Hall as a joke, and for some reason the name had stuck.

"No light show tonight?" Riley asked, stepping out of the shadows.

She smiled, tempted to amuse him by making the water dance to her tune. But she was tired, too tired for simple tricks. "Did you…" her words trailed off the moment she spotted Donovan, and she eyed Riley with a sense of dread. "Can you give us a minute?"

"Sure. I was headed in to dig out some grub. Your boy here worked up quite an appetite." He jogged up the steps without looking back; the message was loud and clear.

"Donovan…I-"

"You don't have to say anything," he cut in, moving to walk past her. He still hadn't looked her in the eye.

In her desperation, she did the only thing she could, she reached out to him. As her hand made contact with his forearm she opened herself to the connection. Donovan's head whipped towards her, his stormy gaze full of surprise.

"We're family, D. I need you to know that, to see that. I'm not good at all this touchy feely crap, and we both know it." Donovan sagged. It damn near broke her heart. "Whatever you want to do, wherever you want to be. I'm good with it."

He moved so quickly she didn't have time to blink, and she was wrapped up in a bear hug. Donovan held on so tightly her bones creaked in protest, but she didn't complain.

You will not cry.

"You're home, Maddy. I can't explain it, but I don't want to be anywhere but here." His words were muffled against her shoulder. "I was free the moment you got into that ring, but this isn't about gratitude."

"Well, okay then." Maddison gave him a quick squeeze. "We understand each other."

"I'm going to take a position with the League." Donovan stepped back, watching her face before he continued. "But when I'm not on rotation, I'll be there to back you up."

"Understood." Maddison turned as he did to mount the stairs. "You'll get a feel for how the League operates tomorrow. We're headed for the Enchanted Realm, so it's all hands on deck."

As they stepped into the grand foyer of Merc Hall, Maddison filled him in. Their footsteps were almost soundless on the smooth marble floor. "Aretha's kingdom is protected by powerful magic. We can't port directly to her realm, so we have to take a detour."

Donovan thought it over. "Surely there's another way to get a message to her?"

"You would think." Maddison shrugged. "The Alliance could, Lucas too probably, but Obadiah is here against orders so he's kind of avoiding the whole reunion thing."

Anger flashed across Donovan's face, anger with a touch of bitterness, but he didn't say anything.

"What is it, D?" She knew, of course, but wanted him to say it.

"All the damn rules. If there's a risk Draco can actually travel to Empyrean, the Alliance should be doing everything in their power to prevent that from happening. Instead they make us all jump through hoops, following rules that don't even make any sense, and we're the ones on the ground getting the shit kicked out of us at every turn."

Maddison waited a beat. "Feel better?" she asked.

His face creased into a smile. "Much."

"Most rules are made to be broken, kid. And we do okay." She thought about Aretha's power. The Fae Queen had earned her right to independence, and the simple truth was, everyone, mortal and immortal alike, played to her tune. It was what it was.

"We've also got backup." Maddison beamed at him. "We both know there will be opposition, it's a given. But we can handle it, right?"

"We?" Donovan raised his brows.

She elbowed him in the ribs. "You're contract's not up yet, buddy, so it's me and you on babysitting duty."

It was good to hear the deep rumbling laugh. A few hunters looked in their direction as they passed through what had previously been a reception area, and was now a recreation room. A huge plasma television dominated the space, surrounded by old, battered couches they had moved from one of the offices.

"What do you think of him?" Donovan asked, pushing through the double doors which led to the first floor corridor and, more importantly, kitchen.

"Obadiah? I think he's hiding something, and it relates to Zara." She glanced to the right, to a room which was now a dormitory and housed one of their newest recruits. The rumblings she heard inside were the beginnings of an argument. It took a second to reach out with her senses. Whatever the hunter had done, Jonas was tearing him a new one. Their commander and chief always came down heavy on their trainees; mistakes could lead to major casualties.

"It's the way he looks at her," she said, continuing down the corridor. "There's history there. I'm sure of it."

Donovan stopped walking. He tilted his head, eyes narrowed on her face. "It's not the reason you're beating yourself up though, is it?" When she narrowed her eyes at him he beamed in response. "You were tempted to report his presence to the Alliance."

After a few seconds, Maddison gave in. The laugh bubbled free before she could stop it. "Damn you're good." She fell into step again. "Is it weird that I suddenly feel the need to play the good little soldier? I have to report it eventually."

"You've always been a good soldier. There were just less rules before." Donovan's voice held a note of pride. "Are you going to invite Riley to the party?"

Riley and Donovan had become fast friends. They were an unlikely duo, but it seemed to work. "I'd be foolish not to. Trouble is Riley's middle name. I'd be surprised if it isn't stamped across his birth certificate."

"Maybe the tattoo is enough."

"When you've finished with the heart to heart, the food's getting cold in here."

Speak of the devil.

The sight of Riley in a chef's apron had her doubling over. The white scrap of material barely covered his heavy bulk. "Nice threads," she said, slanting him a grin when he growled at her. "Lighten up, wolf-man. I have something for you to sink those teeth into." A plan was already forming in her mind. She knew exactly where she'd place Riley in the field. As a scout there was nobody better. They could use his skills.

"Then by all means, step into my kitchen."

Said the werewolf to the witch.

Maddison took a deep breath of hot simmering spices as she entered the room. Riley had cooked his famous chilli. Her stomach growled in anticipation the moment she spotted the covered pan on the stove. "I take it Donovan's not the only one who worked up an appetite. She pulled out a stool at the long counter. "Dish it up and you can tell me all about it."

"Don't be a tease," Riley said, walking to the stove. "I want to know what was better than facing off with a Sentinel demon." He accepted a bowl from Donovan, spooning a generous helping before moving onto the next.

"Okay, fine. But only because you're feeding me." Maddison tucked her boots under the bottom rung of the stool and started from the beginning.

Thirty minutes later she was laying out the weapons she needed on her bed. If she was lucky, she could grab a few hours before it was time to meet Zara and the others. They had spoken on the phone, or argued was more accurate. Especially when Maddison learned of the attack on Zara's Ward. Maddison didn't doubt Zara was in good hands. Sebastian was with her, which meant Zachariah would not be far behind. It also meant Maddison wouldn't get the chance to speak with her partner before the assignment.

A chill skittered across her skin, setting off her internal alarm. *No. No. No.*

Maddison turned, shielding her eyes from the ball of light which began in the centre of the room, and expanded outwards until she saw into the heart of it. How could a man with such darkness in him produce so much light? She wondered, staring into Orion's obsidian eyes.

After a second of tense silence, one Orion normally felt the need to fill with useless words, his eyes dropped to the sword on the bedspread.

"You must stop this foolishness, Maddy. You're going to get yourself killed."

Maddison was so stunned, all she could do was gape at him.

"There's a war coming, and you do not want to find yourself in the middle of it."

"I'll take that under advisement." Maddison's internal alarm was ringing so loud it made her head spin.

Orion was fast. He whipped the chair away from Maddison's desk, and forced her into it; all at the flick of the wrist. Her body obeyed, though she still had the use of her limbs, so there was that. For some reason, Orion's powers were limited on her.

There was no humour in him tonight, no playful teasing. It terrified her. Orion was truly worried. What it had to do with her, Maddison had no idea. She was under no illusions he actually cared.

It was odd to watch him pace like a caged beast. Not once in all the time she'd known him had he betrayed such emotion. "What aren't you telling me?"

Orion paused, his whole body stilling.

Why do I feel like the tiger just found his prey?

"Draco has guards stationed throughout the Enchanted Realm. You're walking into a trap."

"We have it covered." She indicated the weapons. "This isn't a hobby. And it isn't why you're here."

"I'm here to talk some sense into you. The Prime will get himself killed and he'll take you with him."

Maddison narrowed her eyes. "Seems to me he's the only one doing something."

"For purely selfish reasons."

"What-"

Orion held up a hand. His fingers twitched, ever so slightly, and Maddison felt the chair begin to move towards him. "Will you stop this foolishness or not?"

"Why do you care? If Obadiah fails, your friend will get exactly what he wants."

"Friend?" Orion laughed. A genuine sound which was oddly pleasing. "Draco does not have friends. And I would rather you make it through this particular fight. You amuse me, Woody. In this life, one needs a little amusement."

Maddison welcomed the power which surged through her body. She shot upright, bursting free of the invisible restraints. "I'm not buying it," she said, kicking the chair back toward the desk. "Either tell me what this is really about or get out."

Commence with the smiting.

There was that damn word again. Yet thoughts of Sebastian led to Zara, and her spine straightened. If Orion was going to kill her, he'd have done it already.

"You don't have the power to move against me. The only chance you'd have is by knocking me out." Orion smiled; a secret smile she recognised. "Even a god will fall under the spell of his ancestors."

Maddison took a step back. "Why would you tell me that?"

Orion's eyes gleamed with humour. "Just remember what I said."

She had to cover her eyes against the explosion of light.

"Until we meet again. Woody." His laughter echoed back at her. The only thing which remained of his presence.

"Why?" Maddison said to the empty space in front of her. "Why would you give me such an advantage?"

It's not an advantage without the right spell.

Her hackles rose when she felt a presence outside her door. Relief quickly followed. It was Donovan.

"I came to see if there's anything you need before I crash for a few hours."

Maddison was already halfway across the room by the time he appeared. "Actually, we need to go see a man about a god. I need a power word, one strong enough to put Orion on his ass."

"I'm not even going to ask."

She patted his arm. "Don't worry, we don't have to go far." There was only one person she could think of when it came to information on the gods. Jonas might be human, but his mind was his weapon. The damn thing was like a super computer. It was time she hacked into it.

SIX

Zara glanced at the clock, convinced the time piece had frozen in place. How could it be only 10pm? So much had happened, and so much was yet to come. She should be checking on Gregory, not waiting to go into battle. He was her Ward, hers to protect.

"What are you thinking?" Obadiah asked, startling her. His voice was low, husky; familiar in a way she didn't like or understand.

"That I should check on my other Wards." It was better than the waiting. The endless minutes of watching the clock, hoping it would tell a different story. "A few live in the building," she said, rising before someone could change her mind. "I should have visited hours ago, but…" Her words trailed off. There was no need to finish the sentence. She had no desire to.

"Why do I get the feeling you're running, Zara," Obadiah asked, making her shiver because it was close to the truth. He shouldn't know so much about her. Yet he did.

Her chin came up, defiance straightening her spine as she walked to the door. "I'm simply doing my job. A quick visit will give me peace of mind."

Sebastian grunted, drawing her attention. Okay, so it was a weak excuse. All she had to do was scan the building to assure herself of their safety. She could do that without leaving the apartment. But she needed to get out. Now.

"Fine. So I need to stretch my legs. It's a better alternative to staring at four walls, because you're not the most communicative bunch."

It was almost funny when they looked at each other from their different positions across the room. Zachariah was brooding about something, so hadn't said more than two words since he arrived. Her brother was pretending to catch up on his reading, and all Obadiah could do was stare at her. Weren't they just the regular dysfunctional little family?

"There's food in the kitchen. Help yourself." With that she hurried out of the door.

The distance didn't help. She could feel Obadiah's presence in every part of the building. Those haunting grey eyes seemed to follow her everywhere. The worst part, was the familiarity. It was an itch under her skin – an awareness of him. He had power over her, and not because of his position.

Still, she could hardly walk up and down the halls like a prison guard, so she called upon those in her care, spending a few minutes catching up on their news.

When she reached Bob Jeffries' door, she felt a sharp twang of pain, instantly followed by guilt. She should have checked in on him earlier.

His pain was acute tonight, she felt it in every cell of her body and had to swallow down the lump which had formed in her throat.

She wasn't supposed to have favourites, but she had a soft spot for Bob; a ninety-eight year old ex-marine who had been diagnosed with pancreatic cancer four years ago. Her assignment was to ease his passing. Even after all their time together, it still felt too soon.

With a deep breath, Zara closed her hand over the door handle and applied the filter before she stepped over the threshold. "Now then, Bob. How're we doing today?" she called brightly.

When Bob squinted through the dim light he saw a middle-aged woman with a generous swish of hips and a handsome, appealing face. He had a soft spot for Zara, and, as usual, she brightened his day.

"About time you showed up, young'un. I've been waiting to thrash you at gin-rummy all day."

Zara noticed the pain behind his words. She absorbed as much as she could to lessen the burden. She wasn't as skilled at healing as her brother. "You old snake, always after my money."

His chuckle turned into a wracking cough. The cancer had spread to most of his body.

She laid a hand on his chest and the coughing eased. "Is the pain bad today, old man?"

It was a running joke, making reference to their age. It was, in her own way, a term of endearment.

"Nothing I can't handle." He gave a watery smile. "Are you going to get the cards, or are you too chicken?"

Zara laughed and walked to retrieve the deck. "Have you eaten?"

"Stop fussing, I'm okay. That's what the carers are for." She knew how much he hated the weakness, or any reminder of what the disease was doing to him.

"Always thinking of yourself. I haven't eaten yet, but thanks for asking."

His chuckle this time didn't set off a coughing fit. "There are leftovers in the fridge. I knew you'd visit hungry, you always do."

"Oh, I could kiss you." She did just that, laughing hard when colour rose in his cheeks.

Two minutes later she was tucking into a mouth-watering lasagne one of the neighbours had dropped in.

She ate as they played cards. It was part of their routine, one which made him feel less like an invalid and more like a caring friend.

"Did you know that Sandra in 3A has herself a new young man?" Bob asked as he played his hand.

"Why do you think I come here? To catch up on all the gossip."

He made a grunting sound in his throat. "She deserves a nice man, our Sandra. She's had a tough time of it."

Zara smiled. He had a good heart. He wasn't nosey by nature; he just cared about the people around him. They had that much in common.

"I couldn't agree more." Her smile deepened. "Have the Edwards' had their baby yet?"

Linda and John Edwards lived in 6C. They were expecting their first child.

"A baby boy, 9lb 8oz – he's a big one."

The coughing started again. Zara automatically reached out, but it was difficult to control the spasms. He was tired. She could see it in every line of his face, but he would never admit it.

She waited another ten minutes, let him win a few hands before she made her excuses. "I need to check in on the repairs in 1B and sort through applications for our latest vacancy. Maybe we could watch a movie later in the week?"

"You're too young to be wasting your time with an old man," he said, but she could hear the relief in his voice. He needed to rest.

"And you're too old to be choosy."

He grinned, trying to fight the heaviness in his eyes. "Okay, but only if I get to pick the movie."

"Deal, I'll bring the popcorn."

"Extra caramel," he shouted as she was closing the door.

The pain started before she'd made it a few steps towards her own apartment. It was a by-product of using her gift, and since she hadn't rested yesterday, she was paying for it now.

Inside the sanctuary of the hallway, she sank to her knees and waited for the worst to pass. She didn't hear Obadiah approach, which showed her how severe it was.

"Zara. What's going on?"

"Nothing," she said through clenched teeth. "Just give me a minute."

She heard him curse and felt his presence beside her. "Tell me what you need."

All she could do was shake her head.

He lifted her then, and the grief eased a little. It felt wrong for her to share the burden, and yet his arms felt too good to deny a little comfort.

"Tell me what's going on," he demanded, when the worst of it passed.

"It's the price of using my gift. When I absorb too much emotion it has a physical side effect. There's always a consequence."

He seemed to consider that, silent for a time as he moved towards the apartment. "So this… tightness, a kind of itching under the skin, that's my human form compensating in some way?"

She nodded, stronger now. "It's normal for the newly Fallen, though you're lucky because the transition is advanced."

"It eases when I'm around you," he said, and she could see he was surprised by the admission.

Interesting.

"I absorb emotions. It's not unusual." It was a lie but he didn't press it, and she was grateful. "It takes adjustment," she said, clinging to a safer subject. "There's a great deal of power within you and your body has to find a way to deal with it. And the brain, too, has a way of rebelling at first, until you find a harmony between body and soul."

"So I'm feeling echoes of the past inhabitant?"

She frowned at his terminology. "There are certain needs, physical and emotional needs, which you adopt as you transition. When you're hungry, or tired, even in a high emotional state, your body will resort to its most basic instincts."

"Is that your explanation for what's happening between us?" he challenged, and her pulse kicked to life.

"I don't know how to answer that," she admitted. "For one, I can't get a read on you and it makes me…uncomfortable."

Obadiah dropped her to her feet outside the apartment door. *'Maybe you shouldn't be so presumptuous.'*

Emotion flooded her at hearing his voice in her head. Her mind recognised him. But how was that even possible? *'I'm not being presumptuous. I have no control over that part of my gift, and the only time my senses fail is when someone is hiding their emotions from me.'* She saw something flash across his face. It looked suspiciously like fear.

'I'm merely trying to protect you.'

'By keeping your emotions on a leash?' She paused with her hand on the doorknob. *'I don't understand why you would feel the need to do that, or the reason you're risking everything for my family-'*

'You,' His mental voice was a caress. *'I risked everything for you.'*

'Why?' Silence filled her mind. She stared down when Obadiah covered her hand with his and turned the knob.

'Because it's my job to protect you.'

"I don't need protecting," she murmured, an echo from a time long past. She had said those words before, hadn't she?

"Your brother and his Watcher are resting. I think we should do the same."

Zara nodded, her mind reeling from the exchange. It was like being in a trance. She didn't even remember saying goodnight. Things became clearer when she was alone in her room, and the sense of the familiar eased her turbulent thoughts.

As she followed her nightly ritual to soothe the nerves fluttering in her chest, Zara tried to make sense of his words. *'I risked everything for you.'* She could still feel the echo of emotion. The pain which bit into her heart.

She glanced at the wall which separated her from the guest room. There was no need to seek out Obadiah's energy. Zara felt it like a charge along her skin. "Who are you?" she whispered, though she feared the answer. The journey to Aretha's realm would surely be fraught with danger, and yet she had the terrible feeling the greatest risk, at least to her, was in the next room.

***

Obadiah felt the effects of a sleepless night in every line of his body. He ached, and most of it was from wanting something he shouldn't – couldn't – have. He'd lain awake for hours, in turn soothed by Zara's presence and frustrated by it. There was so much distance between them. He hadn't been this close to her in hundreds of years, and it evoked memories he couldn't afford. Not if he wanted to keep his sanity.

When he heard movement in the next room he forced himself to get out of bed and move towards the shower. The hot spray eased his aching limbs. In truth, he healed quickly now. His body didn't require the rest. His mind did.

Still, he spent far longer than he should under the powerful stream. It was oddly soothing, and masked the ache he was beginning to associate with his proximity to Zara. It was only when he sensed her reaching out to him, searching his mind, that he shut off the spray and climbed out.

He grabbed a towel from the rail and slung it around his hips. It was a novelty, primitive acts such as brushing his teeth and grooming himself. He could have used his power to save time, instead he wiped steam from the mirror and learnt what it was to be human.

When he walked back into the bedroom he came up short at the sight of Zara in the doorway.

She was dressed in no-nonsense black combat trousers and a khaki shirt two sizes too big. His mouth watered. She was beautiful. In any form she took.

It had always been this way between them, an almost magnetic pull. She didn't remember it, but she felt it now. Her eyes roamed down his body and back up to his face. The stark hunger in her expression made his pulse jump.

"You like looking at this form," he said, his voice low and husky.
"Yes."

Her honesty surprised him, heated his already burning skin. It made sense now, her desire to access his thoughts, because he certainly wanted to know what was going on it that pretty head of hers. He shouldn't have done it, but he reached out to take a peek. Saw that she was thinking about kissing him again, about biting into the flesh of his bottom lip and tasting him.

"Do it," he said in challenge, and was across the room before he'd even processed the thought.

He bent forward so she had access to his mouth, his impatience humming in his blood as he waited for her to act on her desire.

"This is crazy," she whispered, closing the distance between them.

The pleasured sound she made lit up his every nerve ending as she bit down on his lip and then licked a line across it. She took her time, savouring, winding her fingers into his hair until she had him exactly where she wanted him.

It was so erotic, the way she feasted on him. "Obadiah," she breathed against his lips, and he felt another crack in his armour. If he allowed her to feel what was churning inside him it would terrify her. She filled his senses. Filled him; heart, body and soul. His need for her was a pain he had no desire to stifle. It kept him grounded.

When she released him, her eyes were dark and turbulent. "Maddy is here," she said, voice husky.

"I think I'm going to kill her." He stepped back, composing himself. "Slowly."

Zara laughed, and the sound was like a punch to his heart. "I'll go round up the troops." She slipped out before he could respond, which was a good thing. It gave him time to process.

When he walked through into the hall he followed his nose to the kitchen, where he found Zara and Maddison at the table. Zachariah was at the stove this time, arguing with Sebastian; something about eggs. Obadiah didn't care, his attention was on the delicious aroma brewing in a pot. It seemed his vessel had a weakness for coffee.

"Hey, Obie," Maddison said, biting into a slice of bacon. His face told her what he thought of the name. She held up her hands, laughing softly. "Okay, okay. Obie is out. But I need to call you something."

"How about you use my name?"

His suggestion was met by a snort. "What would be the fun in that?" Maddison shrugged. "We'll think of something."

Obadiah poured coffee into a mug and took it to the table. "Will we now?"

"Absolutely." A lighting fast grin. "But let's get down to business. We'll go directly to Tobias' domain, and from there we'll travel to the portal at the far side of Firmani. It shouldn't take more than a day."

He listened intently as she laid out the plan, and could find no fault in it. It still irritated him, the missing piece of the puzzle. There was a blank spot in his mind when it came to Maddison; a knowing he couldn't quite reach.

"Where's Donovan?" Zara asked, scowling when Sebastian piled more food onto her plate.

"He went ahead with Riley. It will save time if Tobias has the plan up front."

Zara's lips twitched. "What? You mean you haven't spoken to him this morning?"

Maddison pulled a face. "I'll be seeing him soon enough." She turned to throw daggers at Zachariah, thankfully it was only with her eyes. "And you can wipe that smug look from your face."

Obadiah cleared his throat. "I think you need to work some of your mojo on our friend here. She's wound tighter than a grysler stick."

Sebastian threw back his head and laughed, whether at reference to the primitive weapon or his comment in general, Obadiah couldn't be sure. Not until he spelled it out.

"Zac's happy vibe doesn't work on her. It seems Maddy has an aversion to feeling good."

"Bite me," Maddison shot back, while all Obadiah could do was stare.

"Explain," he demanded, feeling for an answer he still couldn't reach.

"I guess you could say magic doesn't work on the witch," Zachariah said. "Though that's not entirely accurate considering what happened with the Carnival sisters."

Maddison and Zachariah shared a smile, which spoke of a history as rich as the one he shared with Zara. Obadiah felt a twinge of envy.

"Powers have a limited effect on me. I have no idea why," Maddison added, turning to him. "Zara can't read me as well as she should, or alter my emotional grid, and Zac can't influence me with his mojo either."

Obadiah frowned. "But how-"

"How does she get me?" Maddison winked at Zara. "She uses her natural intuition, or her powers of friendship, to wheedle information out of me."

"What about others. Are there any instances where power can influence you?"

Maddison's eyebrows crunched together as she contemplated his question. "There's Orion Reece. His parlour tricks don't have any effect, but he has certain power over me."

The name had alarm bells ringing in his head. But why? Reece was a power house, so Obadiah would have been more concerned if they had no control.

"We should get moving," Sebastian said, rousing him from his thoughts.

When Obadiah looked up, Maddison was watching him. To cover the awkward tension between them, he pushed back from his chair.

"You're right. We should."

He stood, watching as Zachariah and Maddison armed themselves. It interested him that they removed their weapons to share a simple breakfast. He wondered idly if it was some hunter rule – no deadly knives at the dining table.

When Zara left, to return a few minutes later with a bow and quiver, a memory hit him so hard and fast it took his breath. Zara was opposed to violence, it was part of her nature; a prerequisite to her empathic gift. Yet, ironically, she had shown the most aptitude in weapons training, especially with a bow. It probably didn't see a lot of action, but it was clear from the way Zara handled the sleek bow she still knew how to use it.

Obadiah held out his hands, inviting Zara and Maddison to form a connection. Sebastian stepped forward a second later, followed by Zachariah and the group formed a circle. It was time.

SEVEN

Three, two, one. Ready as I'll ever be.

But Maddison wasn't ready. Not even close. As they arrived on the border of Aronmyre, the sight of Tobias shattered her defences; the dark, lethal force of him. It was like a blow. Add in the beautiful backdrop of his land, as large and virile as the king himself, and she had to throw up every shield she had.

Had it been this way before? She wondered. Before they had shared a bond. Maddison didn't want to answer the question, even to herself. His guard of three were in position; two in the air and one on the ground. Maddison also spotted several members of the League, in addition to Riley and Donovan, who had brought a few friends of their own.

She stepped away from her group, strolling towards Tobias with more confidence than she felt. Their gazes clashed, locking in a way both familiar and frightening.

'Are you avoiding me again, Maddison?' She heard the deliberate growl in her head.

'I'm here, aren't I?'

Tobias didn't respond. He didn't speak again until she was directly in front of him. "Everyone is in position, per your request." His lips twitched. "Is there anything else you require?"

"There are enough chiefs at this particular party, so don't get all high and mighty. You know I appreciate your help."

'Prove it.' Tobias let it hang for a second. "I sent scouts ahead, but so far I've had nothing specific. Just reports on increased activity."

Maddison looked over her shoulder, where the others held back; watching them with interest. "That's why Riley's here. He spots trouble from a mile away." She looked up. "And then there are the twins. Your eyes in the sky."

Tobias laughed softly. "You've called them worse."

She inclined her head in acknowledgement, and glanced to her left. Marcus, the leader of Tobias' three, took it as an opportunity to show off. He transformed into a broomstick. A god damn broomstick she seethed, ignoring the tug of amusement.

Marcus was a talented shape-shifter; a skill all hympes possessed, but one he turned into an art form.

Maddison stepped forward, biding her time until Marcus returned to his true form. She allowed her hair to reach out and slide across his chest in a provocative movement. "Are you flirting with me, Marcus?"

The colour drained from his face so fast she almost betrayed her amusement. He actually took a step back.

A laugh erupted from Tobias' chest. "You deserved that one, my friend."

Maddison turned away to hide her smile, recoiling her wayward mane. "I'd like you to meet-"

"Obadiah," Tobias interrupted, stepping forward. "It's an honour to welcome you to my home."

She watched the two men curiously as they made their introductions.

"I don't like this," Marcus said from behind her; a little too close for comfort. "If anything happens to Tobias because he has a compulsion to-"

Marcus didn't get the rest of his sentence out. Maddison's hair whipped out, and this time she wasn't gentle. She knocked him back two steps.

Donovan and Riley were beside her in an instant. "Easy boys," she said, her eyes never leaving Marcus. "Tobias controls the League, and to ask him not to lead his men would be an insult." Her words were pitched so only he could hear. They had already drawn too much attention.

In truth, Maddison understood Marcus' position. It was his duty to protect his king; a king who would never sit on a throne or delegate his duties. It wasn't who Tobias was.

"It's time," Zachariah said, walking into the fray with an easy grace Maddison had always admired. No doubt he was pumping enough happy juice into Marcus to make him drunk on the feel-good vibe.

The group wasted no time disbanding. It was a coordinated effort. They knew exactly what was expected, and set off in the direction of Firmani. Marcus hung back as he coordinated with the twins in the air.

Naturally, Riley was in the lead, following Tobias' instructions. The route he'd chosen took them through the forest which surrounded Aronmyre. It would take almost a day to navigate to the first border point.

Maddison found an easy rhythm. Her steps synced perfectly with Donovan's as she kept her senses tuned to the environment, never letting Zara out of her sight. The scenery didn't hurt. Tobias' land was resplendent with plants so varied in their species they were a constant delight. The trees, tall and foreboding like great giants of the forest, could only be found in this section of the Enchanted Realm.

She had heard the stories, the ones of Tobias' ancestors; a grandfather of centuries gone by who had planted the protectors of Aronmyre to signify each year he had spent within the trials. They signified a rebirth, and every heir to the throne continued the tradition.

She knew Tobias had honoured the tradition, though she had yet to discover the location. His years during the trials, the torture he'd endured, had broken others of his kind. Not Tobias. The moment he broke free of his chains, he had established the Enchanted League and accepted his rightful place as leader of his people.

'What are you thinking about, Watcher?'

Maddison turned to look at Tobias as his words filled her head. He had taken to using the name, and in truth she didn't mind it. *'You.'* She watched his eyebrows shoot up in surprise. *'I'm wondering where you planted your offering to Aronmyre.'* Tobias' jaw clenched, the amusement sliding from his face so quickly Maddison regretted her question. He was silent for almost a minute.

'Maybe I'll show you one day.'

This time it was Maddison's turn to be surprised. His tone so intimate she felt a blush working its way across her cheeks.

You deserved that.

"I don't like this," Donovan said beside her. It gave her the perfect out.

"This is Tobias' land. I doubt the Fractured want to take him on without an advantage." Maddison smiled, without humour. "It would be a declaration of war."

Donovan pulled a face. "So what you're saying is. The moment we step out of Aronmyre all bets are off?"

"I wouldn't put it like that." Maddison looked up to the sky. "Not with the deadly duo up there, and Riley watching our back.' Riley missed nothing.

Despite her words, Donovan's unease began to settle around her, until she could no longer see the beauty in her surroundings; the lush greens and exotic colours which could be found nowhere in the mortal realm.

They stopped as darkness began to fall; night pushing against them to mix with the tension in the air. Tobias made the decision to camp, two miles from the edge of his land. There was a brief discussion about how they would roster up watch duty. Surprisingly, nobody complained about sharing the load. They were now a unit and were behaving as such. Of course, the siren twins, who remained in bird form, had a distinct advantage; their senses were attuned to the environment even as they slept.

"It's dropped a little cold," Zara murmured, rubbing her arms. Her eyes turned mischievous. "Care to help out with that?"

Maddison grinned at the question, removing a gold band from her hair and dropping it to the soft grass. She held her hand directly above it, allowed the aquilliam to extend at her command. It was an elfin metal, a gift from Michael. When it was large enough for the desired result, she shot power into the ground; stepping back as flames erupted from the circle. Maddison could control all elements to a certain degree. It was part of her gift; one she didn't question.

"Showing off, witch?" Marcus said from the other side of the circle.

Maddison flicked her wrist so the flames exploded outward in his direction. Marcus leapt back instinctively, though this particular magic didn't burn. It would preserve the earth. "That would be showing off," she answered, turning away.

To his credit, Marcus laughed good-naturedly at Tobias' exasperated, "Will you two behave?"

Since Maddison was on second watch, she wasted no time settling herself in a comfortable position on the ground. There would be no ghost stories around the camp fire for this group. They knew the monsters were real, and they would face them soon enough.

Donovan took up position beside her; head palmed on his hands as he stared at the sky.

"Don't they need a break too?" he asked.

Maddison followed his gaze to the twins, their graceful bodies hovering; pale feathers glinting against the dark. "They'll land soon," she told him, eyes fluttering shut. "Get some sleep, D. It won't be long until you see a little action."

He grunted. "I think you're confusing me with pretty boy." It was his name for Riley, and he wasn't wrong. With his dark skin and sinful eyes he was truly beautiful. In wolf form, all his glossy black hair transformed into the colour of a night sky.

"Riley lives for the hunt, it's true. But even our wolf is restless tonight."

Donovan didn't ask how she knew that. It was part of Maddison's power; the connection she felt to her friends. She could have told him about her concern for Zachariah because, even now, she could feel his unrest. It had nothing to do with the assignment. Her brother was hurting, and when it was over, she would find out why.

The next thing Maddison became aware of was the gentle pressure of fingertips against her shoulder. When she opened her eyes she found Obadiah looming above her.

"You're up," he said quietly, dropping his eyes. "Care to release me?"

Maddison smiled as she uncurled her braid from around his wrist. The sirens weren't the only ones who remained vigilant in their sleep. They were all soldiers in some form or another.

In order for Maddison to maintain the power it took to control their would-be camp fire, she had to remain close to the surface, even a rest. The flames were low now, as though the embers were dying out.

"Anything to report?" she asked Obadiah, as he curled himself in front of the flames; eyes on Zara.

"Not a thing."

He almost sounded disappointed. But Maddison wasn't fooled. They were all feeling the tension; all waiting for the inevitable. "How do you know her?" she asked instead, following his gaze.

Obadiah took so long to answer she feared she had spoken out of turn. It was easy to forget hierarchy when they were fighting side by side – or not as the case seemed to be. For how long remained to be seen.

"We trained together."

Maddison's brows shot up. His voice was pitched so low the words carried away in the cool night air. "I'm guessing there's a reason she doesn't remember."

The sound he made was so close to a snort she had to bite her lip to prevent a smile. It seemed so alien, so out of place, and she didn't even know him. "Will you tell her?" Maddison didn't ask why his memory was still intact. She doubted he would divulge such information to a relative stranger.

"It is forbidden." Obadiah paused to glance into the flames. "But I will share what I can."

Maddison heard the words left unsaid; the emotional resonance was clear. Obadiah cared deeply for her friend. Her gaze flickered to Zara, and she felt a sliver of sympathy, of loss, on her behalf. "You can see into this realm. That's how you know so much." It wasn't a question.

"I have that ability." He smiled. "Though you could say I overuse it."

"Have you remembered what it is you know about me yet?" Obadiah turned to her, the surprise evident in his eyes. She shrugged. "You get this look. It's like you're trying to remember something important."

"I can't find the missing piece," he admitted. "But even if I could, I might not be able to share it."

Maddison nodded in acknowledgement of the warning. It had something to do with Orion Reece, she was sure of it.

EIGHT

Tobias took the last watch. He hadn't really expected an attack, but he couldn't shake the feeling that trouble was right around the corner.

'Do you see anything?' he asked Melia without looking up. Tobias knew she was feeling restless, so he didn't reprimand her for ignoring his earlier command.

'No, Sire. But I'm going to take a wider sweep.'

'Understood.'

The flames drew his gaze, the fire that wasn't really a fire. It moved something in him that Maddison protected the earth; the home of his ancestors. The heat, which had sustained them through the night, would leave no evidence behind. Tobias knew she had to be on the edge of consciousness; resting and yet not truly asleep. Maddison was a soldier. She had trained her body to survive under the harshest of conditions. It didn't matter that her earlier experiences had shaped her desire to push herself; it was already part of who she was.

'I can feel your eyes on me, half-blood.'

Tobias loved the sound of her mental voice. She was right about the attention, though he couldn't say when his focus had shifted. *'You feel it too, don't you? The unrest?'*

'I felt it the moment we began our journey. They're watching us. Waiting.' Maddison opened her eyes; the shimmering flames of green reflected by the fire. *'We knew the risks. Draco would do just about anything to prevent us from reaching our goal.'* She stretched out the kinks, her movements almost feline in nature. "What does a girl have to do to get coffee around here?" she said, rising in a fluid moment.

"You're the witch, just say the magic words." Tobias threw her a lazy smile, along with the backpack which was within reach. "Be sure to share the goods."

"I'll second that," Donovan said, so in tune with Maddison he was already coming to his feet. He dipped into the bag to retrieve the small pan, and canteen of water.

Tobias sat back to watch in fascination as the pair worked seamlessly side by side. By the time the others stirred, Maddy had several steaming cups of coffee lined up. She hadn't used her magic once, if you didn't count the heat generated to boil the water.

The coffee was delicious, which was more than Tobias could say for the energy bar they had for breakfast. Still, there was a certain pleasure in sharing the space with this particular group.

They were refreshed and ready to go within thirty minutes of waking; all eager to meet the threat head on. Riley took the lead, his wolf so close to the surface he kept mostly to himself.

After a few minutes, Marcus fell into step beside him. "Melia didn't find anything, which is more worrying than if she had." Marcus' voice was low. "We'll hit Firmani in about twenty minutes."

"Plenty of places to hide," Tobias commented, thinking of the cave system which bordered the stretch of land between Aronmyre and Durin Mountain.

Tobias' sense of dread returned. It didn't make him feel any better that there was no sign of life across the border. To their left the caves loomed like stone giants, casting shadows along their path. The trees here were harsher; like ghosts of their former selves. With little light, coupled with the hard dry land, they had withered; become skeletons with spindly branches and gnarled, twisted roots.

Most avoided Firmani because it was a demonic watering hole; only the deadliest species survived.

Tobias had an uncontrollable urge to fall back, to regroup and choose another path. He turned to seek out Maddison, and when their gazes locked, he saw she was experiencing the same emotion. If they continued, it would amount to walking into a trap.

'Sire.' Melia's voice compounded the feeling of dread. 'Riley has encountered a group about three hundred metres ahead. We're going in to check it out.'

'Understood.'

A trickle of apprehension ran down Tobias' spine. It was the only preparation he got before all hell broke loose. A team of at least two dozen appeared to Maddison's right; a mixture of Lechens, Sidlur, and the repulsive Savingore demons.

'It's a decoy. We're under attack.'

Tobias watched as Maddison surged forward with a dagger in each hand, ready to meet the deadly warriors head on. Somewhere in his brain, it registered how magnificent she looked; green eyes gleaming, long, graceful limbs poised and ready.

But the soldier in him was already assessing the group to find a weakness. The Savingores had a hard shell-like exterior, which rebuffed most metals. Maddison knew the score. She slid to the ground in a show of acrobatics and sliced down the skin of a stout pair of legs.

Tobias noticed his second then, and Marcus was in trouble. He was surrounded by three Lechens; one had its large fangs buried in his forearm, as the others moved with an unearthly fluidity to surround him.

"Hey! Parasite." Tobias moved to intercept, taking control of the closest demon's mind so that he changed trajectory and leapt onto his comrade instead. The Lechen's mind was strong, wilful, so although Tobias could usually control at least two with relative ease, this time he doubted his ability to maintain the hold. Sweat broke out on Tobias' forehead as he struggled. These demons, like the vampire, needed blood to survive; these three had fed, and recently.

It was part of Tobias' gift, the ability to control and manipulate living organisms. The Lechens at full strength were a formidable enemy.

Satisfied Marcus had things under control, he released the mind to enter the fight. The one to step forward had murder in his eyes; a level of bloodlust which told Tobias the group were being manipulated – turned into a machine for the purpose of war. Adrenaline pumped through his system as he understood the danger they represented.

It kept him alert, allowed him to call on the training which had prepared him for the speed of the Lechen race. Zachariah had helped with that. Vampires were descendants of both the Lechen and the Enraptured – the result of a curse which led to a new species. This particular demon wasn't as fast as Zachariah, and he lacked focus and discipline, but he still got a few licks in. Unlike vampires, the Lechen had claws too. Tobias had an open wound on his chest to prove it.

He retaliated, using his short blade to stick the son of a bitch in the gut and, distracted now, the Lechen never saw the next blow coming. Tobias sliced his dagger across the demon's throat; its blade so sharp the effort was negligible. It had been a gift from Maddison.

As the Lechen dropped to the ground he scanned the group. His heart almost stopped when he saw Maddison lying motionless with an arrow protruding from her shoulder.

There are more of them.

A rain of arrows hit the shield Obadiah was struggling to hold. Tobias' gaze shot to the sky. The twins swooped towards the closest archer; their form changing until they were part-woman, part-bird, all terrifying.

'How are you doing, Watcher?'

Nothing. No caustic sarcasm, no arrogant come back. There was just…nothing. Tobias narrowed his eyes, searching her body. He was too far away, and Maddison was too still. His blood turned to ice in his veins until he swore there was a layer of frost along his skin.

His focus honed in on Maddison as he charged across the clearing, slicing down anything in his path; blood coated his upper chest, but he didn't care if it belonged to him or the enemy.

By the time he reached her, Donovan had Maddison's head cradled in his lap. Tobias' hands itched with the desire to scoop her up. The unveiled panic in Donovan's eyes stopped him.

"Tobias!"

He turned to see a Sidlur demon baring down on him. An arrow burst through one of its three eyes. Zara lowered her bow, chest heaving in relief when the Sidlur hit the floor.

Tobias nodded. "Thanks. I-"

The ground rocked beneath his feet, accompanied by the tell-tale sound of approaching footsteps. Tobias spotted Riley, and the wolf was in bad shape. But before he could call out to ask what was coming, Rheia came to land in front of him.

"Sire, there are twelve Nrikabats headed this way."

"Son of a bitch." Tobias swung back to Donovan. "Stay with Maddy."

You have got to be kidding me.

The ground pitched and fell, throwing Tobias off balance. His brain caught up a beat later; they were no longer on the Firmani Trail. They were in Derrymore, the heart of elfin territory.

Tobias' gaze shot to Obadiah, appreciation forming on his lips until he caught the Prime's expression; bewilderment.

Marcus kindly vocalised for them. "What the hell?" They had transported, en masse to the centre of the Enchanted Realm. That took an enormous amount of power.

Sebastian and Zachariah hurried to Maddison's side. The moment Sebastian saw the arrow he choked out a surprised breath. "That's not possible."

"What?" Tobias searched his face, wondering why the hell he hadn't begun to heal Maddison already.

"The arrow…"

Tobias squinted, but didn't see anything unusual – other than the fact the elfin suit around the wound on Maddison's shoulder was beginning to turn black. "What the hell, Sebastian?"

"It's from the bow of Lokheira."

"How can that be?" The bow belonged to a god of old. It had no place in this realm, and was certainly no weapon a member of the Fractured should yield.

"The arrows are poisonous." Riley growled low in his throat. "So I suggest we do something other than howl at the moon. We don't have much time."

Tobias turned to Rheia. "Find out how far we are from the House of Gilliford."

"We're here." Zachariah was already marching toward what appeared to be, at least to the naked eye, a sheer rock face.

Reaching out with his senses, Tobias felt the magic before he saw the ripple of it. He watched as Zachariah touched his hand to a space in front of the rock, and the mirage slipped back to reveal the grand entrance to the House of Gilliford.

The door, which stood at least eight feet high and shimmered in the light, swung open.

Tobias bowed immediately. "Kian."

The elf bowed in return; his tall stature at least 7ft 3. His amber coloured eyes flickered past Tobias to land on Maddison. Kian's expression changed from cool control to heated panic. He stepped forward, ignoring Donovan to place a hand on Maddison's forehead.

"This way." His tone was hurried, his next words spoken in a language Tobias hadn't heard in decades. The tongue of the ancients.
Protect my daughter.

The shock barely even registered. Tobias' every protective instinct was screaming at him to deny the terror in Kian's voice. Maddison couldn't die. He simply wouldn't allow it.

They entered a hallway so bright it seemed impossible there were no windows. The ceiling was high above them; Tobias could barely make out the intricate design from his cursory glance. But he didn't care about the smooth crystalline surface of the walls, or the landings which circled his head and stretched endlessly upwards. His entire being was focused on Maddison; waiting, hoping for a sign she would survive.

Kian led them into a cavernous room, which seemed to spring to life the moment he stepped inside. Darkness fell from the space to reveal a large circular bed in colours of forest green.

Like her eyes.

The walls were uneven, each containing deep ledges of varying heights and diameters; at least two were adorned with a padded material which indicated they were used as a seating area.

Kian walked to one of the ledges and reached inside. A lip shot out, deep enough for storage. Tobias saw why when Kian pulled out a shimmering fabric of palest gold, before instructing Donovan to place Maddison on the bed.

Tobias stepped forward, conscious of the others hovering in the doorway. Zara was already curled up next to Maddison on the covers, stroking her hair and murmuring softly; words he didn't catch.

It was a testament to Tobias' control when he didn't put a restraining hand on Kian's shoulder as he removed the arrow. Already the infection was spreading. The suit she wore had turned a metallic grey around the wound as though, like Maddison's flesh, it was dying.

Tobias held his breath, his eyes watchful, his heart beating heavily. Now that someone else had taken control, Donovan was pacing beside the bed, his gaze shifting from Maddison to the door and back again, as though he wanted to run. It was as distracting as hell, yet Tobias understood his distress.

Kian handed the gold sheet to Zara. "Cover her."

She obeyed without comment, covering Maddison's body until all that remained were her shoulders and head.

Kian grunted something, his concentration absolute. He pressed his fingertips to a spot below Maddison's collarbone, and Tobias' throat went dry. Kian had removed the suit. Tobias' gaze immediately focused on the blood, which marred the golden skin of her left shoulder. Not enough that it hid the ink; a brand on her flesh which he recognised as the Gilliford crest. It was the source of the suits magic, and proved it was an integral part of her.

Tobias turned his head at the sounds of confusion behind him. Three women entered the room, each carrying a tray of supplies; making them the family healers. They moved with quick efficiency, clearing the area around the bed until Tobias found himself shoulder to shoulder with Zara and Donovan, as they each kept an eye on the proceedings.

Donovan turned to him, his eyes haunted. "She's not answering me. It's so quiet. Her mind is so quiet."

His voice was hoarse when he finally found the words. "It's a protective instinct. Her shields are incredibly strong. It doesn't mean anything." But even as he said it, Tobias' gaze dropped to Maddison's hair; the long plait lying dormant against the green pillow. He'd seen the life in those dark, shiny tresses, and yet he saw no indication of it now.

"She'll be fine," he said, to no one in particular.

Don't make me out to be a liar, witch.

***

Maddison stared into the deep blue of the ocean, wondering at the familiar pull which resonated within her very soul. She froze the instant she sensed she was no longer alone.

"My sister." Words spoken in the old language.

Heart exploding in her chest, Maddison spun towards Michael. The sight of him made her chest ache. It had been too long. Too damn long.

Her gaze roamed his short silver hair, locked on to the white gold of his eyes, and then she was running. Michael moved too, slowing his pace when Maddison reached him so he could catch her in his arms.

"I've missed you so much." She buried her face against his neck as she revelled in the familiarity of him. Only with Michael could she let down her guard. His powerful arms held her steady. The warrior body at odds with the gentleness of his heart. Like many of his kind, her brother was tall. He stood at just over seven feet, so her own body was dangling in his tight grip; her boots several inches from the ground.

"I missed you too."

Maddison frowned at the familiar tension in his voice. She'd heard it once before, many years ago. The memory hit her like a slap. "I'm sick."

The demon who had held them for nine pain-filled months had beaten her for disobeying him. Broken and bloody, she had locked herself away behind the deep recesses of her mind. Michael had brought her here. This is where he had found her the last time.

She loosened her hold so Michael was forced to release her. "How bad is it?"

His eyes turned sad. "You were poisoned. Father did the best he could. The rest is up to you."

Tobias.

"What of Zac? Donovan…the others?"

Michael's lips curved slightly. "Sitting vigil."

She stepped back, resisting the urge to pace, though the restless energy ignited her bones. "You have to convince them to continue, Michael. They'll listen to you, and we don't have time for this."

"They're worried about you."

"They can be worried about me somewhere else." Maddison rolled her eyes at his knowing grin. "They can use the anger…wait. How did we get from Firmani to Derrymore?"

Michael placed a hand on her arm, settling her in a way few could. "It would appear you have powerful friends."

"Lucas?" Maddison shook her head. The angel was a stickler for the rules, so it didn't make sense for him to intervene. "Obadiah?"

"A Prime has the power for such a transportation, but not trapped as he is inside the vessel. We don't know who to thank for the intervention."

Now Maddison began to pace. "It had to be Orion. It's the only explanation."

"What passible motive would he have for saving you?"

You amuse me, Woody. In this life, one needs a little amusement. "Who knows with Orion?" She stopped, turned to face him. "Aretha needs to know what's coming, and I won't be responsible for failing this mission."

Michael stepped forward, bending to touch his forehead to hers in the way of the elves. "What is it you would like me to do?"

She smiled, drawing strength from the contact, from the brother of her heart who had seen her at her most vulnerable. "Come." Her hand dropped to fit in his. "Let's walk, and I'll tell you what to say to make it count."

His musical laughter filled the air. "It's been too long, Woody. Please come back to us."

Maddison squeezed his hand. "I'll work on it."

They walked along the pebbled beach, a detail she added because she could. This was a place deep inside the walls of her mind, one Michael had guided her to; a gift. It was a safe haven.

NINE

Zara couldn't take her eyes from the elf with pupils the colour of purest gold. Michael commanded attention, drew it without question. But it was his connection to Maddison she found the most compelling. Zara knew little of their history, other than Michael and Zachariah were the only family Maddison spoke of.

Kian had been gentle with his son, sharing the news of Maddison's injury as though Michael might break. Instead of falling apart as his father seemed to expect, Michael had taken a seat beside Maddison's bed. There, he had placed one hand on her forehead, and with his head bent low in concentration, he had remained for the last twenty minutes.

Zachariah stood by his friend's side, a hand placed lightly on his shoulder as though lending his strength. It was a powerful scene. Nobody spoke; they barely even breathed.

A collective sigh travelled through the room the moment Michael lifted his head. He nodded at Zachariah, who stepped aside to let him up.

Michael walked directly to Zara, the silver hue of his eyes burning into hers. "I have a message for you." His voice was soft, almost musical.

"You spoke to Maddy." Zara didn't question the ability. The bond Michael shared with her was almost tangible.

"She would like you to continue on without her." Michael held up a hand to pre-empt an interruption. "Before you protest. Maddy wanted me to remind you of the consequences should you fail this mission."

Michael turned to Donovan, who was pacing at the foot of the bed in a way which reminded Zara so much of Maddison she had to smile.

"You're to take her place as Watcher," Michael said, surprising them both. "It's important to Maddy to be able to rely on her family, so she must be able to count on you now."

Michael walked to intercept Donovan. He placed a hand on his shoulder, and showed no response when Donovan tried to shrug it off. There was a beat or two of silence before Donovan relaxed.

"Do not let her down." Michael's voice was quiet, compassionate. "Brother of her heart."

Tears burned Zara's eyes as she watched Donovan's body sag. How could he refuse such a request?

"This time you get to fight for her."

Donovan's face paled at Michael's words.

"She plays dirty." Zara blinked away the tears. "But she's right." She turned to glance at Tobias who sat unmoving in one of the alcoves at the back of the room. He hadn't spoken in almost an hour; his attention focused solely on the bed. It was as if, should he turn his attention elsewhere, Maddison would slip away.

Michael followed her gaze, his thoughts aligned with hers. "We can afford to send two of our elite to aid you in your journey."

It was unlikely Tobias would be joining them, or so Zara thought. But when his dark eyes met hers she saw the defiance in them.

"That won't be necessary." Tobias stood, and for once he wasn't the tallest man in the room. His presence still demanded respect. "I need a moment alone with her."

Michael bowed his head. "I'll prepare the necessary provisions for your journey." He walked out of the room without saying anything further.

When Zara turned to Donovan she saw he was bent low, murmuring something in Maddison's ear.

"You tell her she'd better find her way back," Zara said, meeting Tobias' gaze. She had absolutely no doubt he would try to reach her as Michael had done. It she knew anything about Tobias, it was that he was determined enough to succeed.

Tobias gave a brief nod, before walking to Donovan. "If she's ordering you around, even as she sleeps, it means she's not going anywhere. It's safe to let her rest."

Donovan's spine straightened. "Yes, Sire." He turned to Zara. "I am yours to command."

"You are nobody's to command." They were words Zara had heard Maddison utter in the past. "But I appreciate your protection." It pleased her when Donovan's lips twitched. "Why don't we go and gather up the troops?"

Donovan nodded, waiting until she turned to fall into step beside her. Zara had to wonder how hard it was for him to walk out of the room, because it was one of the hardest things she'd ever done.

***

It was easier than Tobias expected to reach Maddison; like Michael had opened the pathways to her mind, enabling others to slip in. It was a shock to see her clothed in a standard hunter's uniform; he'd rarely seen her wear anything but the suit.

She had her back to an ocean of deep, endless blue. It was an odd contrast to the storm of emotion he saw brewing within the light of her eyes.

"What took you so long, half-blood?"

"Funny. I was going to say the same to you. Why are you hiding out here?" He wanted to touch her. But even if he could, this version of her was a mirage.

As if to demonstrate his thoughts, the ocean dropped away and they were standing in a forest akin to the one on his land.

Tobias watched her, waited for her to react. Disappointment flooded him when she only looked back at him; her stare a wicked green.

"You've caused quite a stir, Watcher." He moved forward a step. "Do you feel like re-joining the party?"

Those eyes that reminded him so much of home looked to the sky. "Are you purposely trying to annoy me?" Her lips curved. "That's brave without your guards."

"Don't flatter yourself, witch. I can fight my own battles."

Maddison's gaze dropped to his. "I'll take a rain check on that. I'm not feeling myself." She turned, and with a wave of her hand they were beside a lake; a replica of his own quiet place in the world. Only they weren't in Aronmyre.

"Michael said I'm supposed to fight, but I'm not sure how."

Tobias froze, taken aback by the vulnerability in her tone. More that she was sharing it with him. "So you're giving up?"

Instead of the anger he'd expected, Maddison shrugged. She walked towards the stones at the edge of the lake, choosing a seat with her back to him.

"Michael showed me how to find this place, how to shut myself away so my body could heal. But I can feel the…virus, or whatever it is. It's attracted to the power, and I'm not sure how to stop it." Maddison turned to him, her face set; her shoulders hunched. "Monsters I can fight, it's what I do. But I'm not sure how to defend against something like this."

Tobias walked to sit beside her, so close his shoulder almost brushed hers. "You fight magic with magic."

She laughed, the sound drifting around him like a caress. "Why didn't I think of that?"

"Why didn't you?" Turning to face her squarely, he searched her profile. "What's really going on, Maddy?"

Eyes the colour of emeralds bore into his. "I'm scared, okay. I recognise the signature and-"

"How is that possible? It's a weapon used by the gods." Tobias' mind reeled. He knew she was powerful, she wouldn't have survived otherwise. But to infer she knew the origin of such power?

"I don't know how it's possible, that's what I'm trying to tell you."

"Okay, so you recognise the danger, however you want to put it. What does your gut tell you?"

Tobias let out a breath. Maddison was using him as a sounding board. His own fear had coloured his emotions, preventing him from understanding the simple truth. She didn't expect anything from him, and yet the fact she had waited for the connection; waited to begin this process of elimination in her mind. It proved how much she trusted him. There was no status between them, she cared not that he was a king; Maddison treated him as her conscience. It was a powerful realisation.

"That I have to let it in." She came to her feet in a burst of energy, her long legs eating up the ground as she paced back and forth. "I could deal with this on a psychological level, so it manifests into my greatest fear." She paused as if amused by the notion.

"What's so funny?"

Maddison actually looked embarrassed by the question. She waved it away, refusing to meet Tobias in the eye as she resumed her monologue.

"Or I could fight it on a physical level, which means I have to find the lock that releases me from-"

"Wait." Tobias held up his hand. "You mean you're stuck here?"

She rolled her eyes to the sky. "Not stuck exactly, but I guess you could say it's all tied together because the fear is keeping me here. I have to find out what it is and accept it, or fight it, or both."

"Just answer me one thing." Tobias stood too. He felt an odd prickle at the back of his neck, and realised it meant he was no longer alone in the room with Maddison. His time was running out. "Are you out of danger?"

"When are we ever out of danger?" She stopped pacing to grin at him. "It might take me out of action for a while, but if this thing was going to kill me then I'd-"

Tobias held up a hand. "I get the point." He gave in to the compulsion to touch her, reaching to stroke his fingers down her hair. "It's so still." The words were meant to be in his head, but in an odd way they probably were.

"My power is needed elsewhere." Maddison closed her hand over his for the briefest moment, and then he was being pushed from her mind. *'See you soon, half-blood.'* Her voice echoed in his head. It filled him with such relief he let out a long pent up sigh, before turning to Marcus. His presence was distinctive, their connection true, so Tobias knew exactly who it was before he turned.

"It's time, Sire." Marcus' gaze dropped to Maddy.

"Don't worry, you'll have your playmate back soon enough." Tobias grinned at his number two, at the impatience which crossed his face. "Your secret is safe with me, Marcus." He walked over to put a hand on his shoulder. "I won't tell her you displayed the slightest hint of concern."

Marcus snorted. "She wouldn't believe you anyway."

They stepped out together, shoulder to shoulder and ready to get back to the mission.

TEN

The journey across Derrymore was surprisingly uneventful. They had no choice but to head for the nearest portal, especially given a group of their size. Zara could feel the quiet reluctance like a pulse along her skin. The emotions were overwhelming; the anger, the fear, the need for justice. And that was only in the immediate bodies around her. She was exhausted, tired from fighting the endless assault against her shields.

Obadiah took her hand, squeezing her fingers lightly. The energy of those around them snapped off, until she could feel nothing but Obadiah's touch; his surprisingly soft skin.

"Thank you." Zara glanced across at him, and for once she didn't want to know what he was thinking or feeling. She was grateful for the respite.

"You need to focus. The Orca Planes are hard to navigate, we need to be ready." Obadiah's voice was firm, chiding almost. The familiarity of the tone so jarring it almost shook something loose. But it was beyond her reach, the memory trapped behind the wall she sensed whenever he was close.

"I can take care of myself." Zara tried to pull her hand free, but Obadiah held firm. "I can cope with a little residual emotion." It didn't matter she was being stubborn; their connection scared as much as it soothed.

"No you can't. You're distracted, and it will cost you if you don't shut it down."

Zara glared at his profile. She had no choice since he had yet to look at her. "Like you do?"

"It's the only way to protect you." Obadiah turned, finally meeting her eyes. "I have no choice."

Zara frowned at his words. But she didn't get a chance to respond. Rheia swooped in to land in front of Tobias. In dual form she was a magnificent creature; the strong supple woman, with powerful wings the colour of warm chestnut. Her feathers were interspersed with black; the trailing edge so white they glowed as though infused with light.

"A group of Orcas are headed this way, Sire." Rheia's attention shifted to Marcus. "A group of five."

Orcas didn't normally attack. In fact they were much more comfortable in the water.

"Be on alert," Tobias said, the order directed at the group as a whole.

Donovan stepped to Zara's right. "Perhaps we should fall back."

"No. We move as a group. We have strength in numbers." Obadiah dropped Zara's hand, moving forward to address Rheia. "Did they have weapons?"

Rheia shook her head. "They're unarmed."

It seemed to reassure the group. Without Obadiah's touch to anchor her, Zara could feel the tension drain from them like a collective sigh. In all except one. Her gaze shot to Riley, her mind honing in on his turbulent energy.

Dark mahogany eyes met hers. Riley's mouth split into a toothy grin. He nodded at her in acknowledgement. The animal close to the surface.

Zara stepped away from the others and walked over to him. She held up her hand, palm facing in, the way she'd seen Maddison do. Riley bent his head in acquiescence, so she put her hand over one muscular forearm.

Zara could almost feel the beast writhing beneath his taught flesh. It calmed within a few seconds.

"If you eat someone, Maddy will be pissed."

She turned at the sound of Donovan's voice, surprised she hadn't sensed his approach.

"You're no fun, Tempest." An orange glow flared in Riley's eyes. "I can promise not to eat a member of the group. How about that?"

"Good enough," Donovan said, laughing at the low growl.

"Play nice, boys." Zara smiled, calmed when the prowling beast beneath her touch settled completely. Both man and wolf were holding it together, so she bent her head in a slight bow before releasing Riley's arm.

By the time the group began moving again, Zara was beside Obadiah as he took the lead. Sebastian and Zachariah, who had been bringing up the rear, were now in the middle of their small unit. Zara felt her senses settle comfortably around her, aided by Zachariah's close proximity. His happy juice, as Maddison liked to call it, was threading its way among them.

It took fifteen minutes to reach the group Rheia had warned about. As soon as Zara saw the Orcas she knew they were going to attack. Their violent intent hit her like a slap; someone had clearly paid for their allegiance.

Without thinking, Zara blasted the first two with a surge of energy, engulfing them in a sea of fear and doubt until they turned on each other in a fit of rage. The effect didn't last long, but it slowed the others down.

Obadiah intercepted the first to break from the line. There was something about the way he moved which struck a chord. During the last attack he had been intent on holding the demons at bay; shielding the group as best he could under the onslaught. Now, he seemed to almost relish the thought of hand to hand combat.

Zara watched as the others surged past her, coordinating so they swarmed on the Orcas. The aquatic creatures were clearly outnumbered and outmatched, yet she could feel their steely determination. It blinded them.

It was almost an unfair fight, until a second group shot from the water directly in their path. Zara dodged out of the way, but wasn't quite fast enough. The Orcas had huge wing-like arms, which ended with sharp claws. One of those arms hit her from the right, lifting her off the ground like a doll. She managed to control her unnatural flight so she didn't smash into the ground on her way back down. She did have a gash in her side, and it stung more than her pride.

"Zara," Donovan shouted as he broke away from Riley and Zachariah.

"I'm okay." She managed to avoid the next attack, but barely. The others had smelled her blood and had her in their sights. "Damn it." She held out a hand and the bow took shape between her fingers. The arrows flew to her as she needed them; a careless use of her power, but she had three Orca's pinned to the ground before Donovan reached her side. None of the shots were fatal. Even knowing they wouldn't show her the same mercy, she hated to kill. Even in defence.

A piercing bark shot through the clearing as an enormous Orca emerged from the lake. His large unblinking eyes pinned her to the ground, and she shivered with the strength of his rage. But it wasn't directed at her, or the group. His wrath was for his soldiers, and she got the impression that whatever she did to them, it would be child's play compared to the punishment he had in mind.

His elongated face erupted into a snarl as he ordered an immediate retreat. The soldiers obeyed without question, slinking back towards the water, each head lowered to reveal the coin sized hole at the top of their skull.

Zara couldn't take her eyes from their leader. She was hypnotised by his powerful gaze.

"We're seeking access to the portal by the Kevlar Fields," Obadiah said, bowing slightly to show thanks for the intervention.

There was a deep rumbling, and a bridge appeared across the water, shimmering in the sunlight.

Beyond the lake, Zara spotted the mountain range, jutting from the earth like a whale out of the water. The bridge would cut their time in half, so she could almost forgive the gaping wound below her ribs.

As though sensing her thoughts, the Orca came forward. His powerful stride shook the ground. He stopped in front of her, raising one arm to reveal a fold at the centre. Zara's breath caught in her throat as he retracted his claws and ran a finger beneath the fold to gather up a line of dark, inky liquid.

She wanted to tell him she healed quickly, but she could see the care he was taking, so she didn't even flinch when he lifted her shirt and ran the finger along her torn flesh. It sealed instantly, though she could feel the burn along her skin.

"Thank you." She bowed as Obadiah had done.

Zara took the responding sound, something between a bark and a wail, to be an apology.

"He told us to hurry," Tobias said, as the Orca walked back to the water's edge and dove into the crystal clear depths.

Zara followed for as long as she could, mesmerised by his strength and speed.

"We only have a few minutes to get across the bridge." Tobias made a signal to his guards. "Let's move out."

In a fluid motion, the group gathered in a line. Zara would have admired the timing if she wasn't still reeling from shock. They filed across the bridge, silent and intent on reaching the other side before they were dropped into the water below.

Nobody spoke for several long, excruciating minutes. They were an hour away from the portal, which accounted for the anticipation buzzing in the air.

Tobias held up a hand. "Let's stop for a breather. We'll know soon enough what's coming."

Zara looked to the sky, and saw the twins in the distance; headed to scout the area ahead. She turned to seek out her brother, and spotted him kneeling beside one of the hunters; healing a nasty gash in his leg.

The sun had begun its steady descent, so Zara knew it would be dark soon. Already, the heavy presence of the mountains on their left cast dark shadows in their path. If trouble was waiting for them at the portal, it would be like fighting blindfolded. Unless you were a wolf. Zara glanced at Riley. He was joking around with Donovan, his mood oddly jovial considering his earlier aggression.

She smiled and walked to sit beneath a small tree; small in comparison to the giants of Aronmyre. After a few minutes, Obadiah came to join her. He handed her a cup filled with warm broth.

"The Orca back there," she said, glancing out towards the lake. "He was important, wasn't he?"

Obadiah didn't immediately respond. He sipped from his own cup; staring into the brown liquid. "He's their general. His name is Moi."

"His intervention. It was because of you?" Zara had seen the reverence in those dark, dark eyes.

"Yes. He sensed my presence…it means I'm running out of time." Obadiah looked at her, his eyes haunted. "Moi's brother forms part of the Alliance."

Zara swallowed the fear which threatened to freeze the words in her throat. "What's going to happen?"

"I don't know. I broke my sacred vow. I intervened when I had no right to."

Silence wrapped around them as Zara digested that. She didn't understand why he was so calm in the face of this new danger.

Obadiah covered her hand with his. "Don't worry. This isn't the first time I've broken the rules, and I doubt it will be the last."

"You say that, and yet…" Zara let her words trail off. There was no point rehashing old ground. Obadiah clearly wasn't going to tell her why he'd risked everything.

"And yet?" he prompted.

Zara shook her head. "Never mind." She drained her cup and stood. "We need to go."

It was easier than Zara thought to convince the others. They all felt the darkness closing in, and didn't have a certain smart-mouthed witch to help light their way. She missed Maddison, not just her company, or her protection, but her unique sense of humour and positive effect on the group. Maddison wouldn't like to hear it, but they all needed the connection.

Tobias communicated with the twins, then gave Obadiah the go ahead to take the lead. It took fifteen minutes to reach Kevlar Wood; colour exploding before them like a pop-up book. The lush greenery had an intriguing violet shade. It lit their way, beating back the growing shadows; a safe haven in the dark.

The path was hidden at first, appearing the moment they stepped onto the trail; a long winding strip of grass sheltered by trees. These were the guardians of the Wood, she knew. If they didn't allow you safe passage, you would be left at the mercy of the creatures who lived below.

Her eyes found Obadiah's as she took another tentative step, unprepared for the branch which shot out to meet her foot. She let out a whoop of delight as the tree limb lifted her from the ground, another already in place for the next step. As she began to walk, finding a natural rhythm, she marvelled at the fact a new shoot was ready to take her weight. Her laughter had a positive effect on the tree spirits, and they began to have a little fun.

They shot her high into the air, catching her before she fell, until she was on a roller-coaster ride – bobbing and weaving along the path. If the thunderous laughter at her back was anything to go by, the others were having just as much fun. By the time they reached the end of the trail, they were all breathless and giddy from the game.

She landed softly and spun to look at Obadiah. A giggle erupted from her throat when she saw a leaf shoot out and swot his behind in a flirtatious gesture. Zara couldn't blame the spirit for appreciating his body.

The smile he gave her was playful and light. It sent her own hormones into overdrive and made her lightheaded.

"Fun looks good on you," she said, returning his smile.

"It looks good on anybody." Tobias laughed, his eyes aglow in memory. "It reminds me of the time…"

She raised her brows expectantly, wondering why he'd stopped.

"Never mind," he mumbled. "We should get going."

They walked in silence for a few minutes until Zara could stand it no longer. "Why do you insist on hiding behind those thick walls?"

she asked, pleased she hadn't made reference to his thick skull. "Considering all you've sacrificed, what would it hurt to let me in?"

Obadiah looked at her, his eyes thoughtful. "Will it make it easier when I'm gone? To know what makes me tick, why I did what I did."

It always came back to that. "None of this is easy. I don't like the fact you're risking your life for me and I don't even know why. There's something between us, I know that you feel it too."

He scowled. "Did anyone ever tell you, you can be extremely annoying?"

"Only you." Zara felt a jolt of alarm, like she'd said the same thing before. Many times. "I wouldn't need to be annoying if you weren't so stubborn."

Obadiah scoffed at the sentiment and went back to walking in silence. Strangely, it wasn't uncomfortable. It was almost companionable.

She turned her attention to their surroundings, charmed by the Golden Barrier - so named for the stretch of natural minerals which reflected the sun and shone like precious metal underfoot. It existed nowhere else, and would turn to dirt on their shoes the moment they left.

"We're close," Tobias said, his strides long, and sure as he caught up to them. "According to Rheia and Melia the coast is completely clear."

Marcus, as ever Tobias' shadow, spoke up. "Which means the surprise party is taking place at the other side."

"It's not really a surprise." Zara felt her brother approaching from behind, with the distinctive energy that could only belong to Zachariah. They were closing ranks, preparing to enter the portal together. It was time for Zara to drop back.

As if on cue, Donovan appeared when she turned; his footsteps matched hers. Obadiah fell into an easy rhythm too, until they were in formation.

ELEVEN

Maddison was aware the exact moment her consciousness returned. She felt the pain in her body like a throbbing pulse beat. Her limbs were like lead weights, pinned to the firm mattress; uncooperative. Docile. The ache in her head travelled all the way to the ends of her hair, which lay dormant against the pillow. Spent.

She didn't have the power reserves to reach out with her senses to scan the room. Not if she was going to try to attack her system from within. To purge the alien power, or as Tobias had put it - fight magic with magic. But this place was as familiar to her as Merc Hall. It was home.

You can do this, Maddy.

It wasn't difficult to reach within to gather her power, collecting it into a tight ball; akin to a fiery knot of tension in the centre of her chest. It burned, and yet it was familiar. Maddison clenched her teeth, squeezed her eyes shut, and let go. The ball exploded, filling her system with hot, bright energy; flooding her cells.

When the light receded she was adrift in a sea of darkness, her mind searching the familiar landscape for any residual poison. Her heart sank when she saw it; a sheen which coated her cells. It did not belong. Maddison concentrated, following its progress for a time, until she understood what was happening. It was not attacking her cells, it was changing them – on a fundamental level.

No.

Her heartbeat was erratic as she let her power settle, let it seep through her body. Instead of a short, sharp blast, Maddison let it coat the alien energy. She felt an immediate reaction; a pressure which radiated in all directions. The frantic rhythm of her pulse was deafening. She understood something else as she fought for control. The foreign power did not want to kill her, it wanted to become part of her, and it was relentless. This weakness in her body was a side effect, nothing more. The new power sought to dominate by stripping away her defences.

Maddison welcomed the surge of anger; so fierce and bright it reminded her of the lost girl she had once been. Alone in the dark, confused and afraid. No more. She grabbed hold of the rage, used it to heat her power, and allowed the inferno to consume everything in its path.

The next time she resurfaced, reclaiming consciousness, she was free. Maddison wanted to weep in relief. Would have done if she hadn't drained every last drop of strength expelling the unwanted power from her system. Her reserves were empty.

She lay for several minutes, floating happily; satisfied with the victory. After a while, she became aware of how vulnerable she was; naked beneath the sheet. Worse, there was someone in the room with her.

Maddison's green eyes snapped open, darting around Michael's chambers to hunt out the presence which was an itch along her skin. She knew that signature; was both terrified and oddly relieved by it.

"I know you're here," she said, her gaze focused at the foot of the bed.

His eyes materialised first; obsidian depths which would have intimidated if they weren't alight with humour. Orion Reece enjoyed to make an entrance, and he dragged it out. "Feeling better, I see." The tone was mocking, though she caught the relief.

Maddison managed a grunt in response. Better was a relative term. Her body had been through the ringer; she could barely lift her head. "Did you come to gloat?" she asked, when he said nothing further. "Now that it appears I'm in your debt once again."

Orion strolled around the bed, pensive. "Consider it a freebie. I'm not even going to say I told you so." He stopped beside her head, holding his palms towards her. "May I?"

She narrowed her eyes at the flames of pale white, which licked along his fingers. "What's it going to cost me?"

"Woody. Woody. Woody." Orion shook his head, exhaling on a long-suffering sigh. "I'm offering my assistance, not bartering for your soul."

Maddison managed a shaky laugh. "Next you'll be telling me you're going to heal me from the goodness of your heart."

The flames at the edge of his finger flared red for a moment. He waved his hands impatiently in a gesture which spoke of his impatience.

Oh what the hell.

She nodded, closing her eyes a second before she felt one of Orion's palms settle on her forehead. The other he placed over her heart. His touch was surprisingly cold. She felt the power like ice running through her veins. But her body surged to life, her cells bursting with so much energy she felt intense nausea roll in her stomach.

When he removed his hands the sickness faded, while the power buzzed along her skin.

I'm like a frigging energiser bunny.

"There she is." Orion's eyes creased with laughter. "And you're welcome."

Maddison waved a hand just below her collar bone, and felt her suit form around her like a second skin. As she threw back the covers and stood, her hair whipped out, stretching as she did. "Thank you."

"There. That wasn't so difficult, was it?" Orion took a step back, glancing towards the door. "But next time, you're on your own. Just so we understand each other."

The teasing note was gone. In its place was his usual arrogance, a sound so familiar she wondered if she'd imagined the rest. "You're not going to tell me why. Are you?"

"Let's just say everyone is where they're supposed to be." Orion winked at her. "And I had some time on my hands to speed up your...recovery."

He began to fade out, the exit as dramatic as his entry. Maddison knew why, she could feel Kian's presence out in the hall too, but she had so many questions.

Good luck with those.

"Maddy!"

Her gaze shot to the door. Kian was staring at her with a mixture of relief and horror creasing his handsome face. She could see Michael in the expression, though their colouring was different. Kian had hazel eyes; a shade so bright they were luminous. His short, spiky tufts of hair were a coppery blonde.

"Father." She moved toward him; her head bowed, her heart full of love.

Kian sighed when their foreheads touched. "I missed you, child of my heart."

Her lips twitched. "But next time I should walk in, right?"

"Should I be concerned that Orion Reece seems to have taken an interest to you?" Kian stood to his full height. "He's dangerous, Maddy."

"I entertain him, or at least that's the story. But I think it's more than that. I don't think he means me harm; in fact, he healed me. It appears I'm valuable in some way." Maddison frowned. "I think he knows more about my past than he would have me believe."

"Come." Kian motioned toward the door. "The others are anxious to see you, and you must be famished." They stepped out into the wide hallway together. "Why do you think his interest is linked to your past?"

As they walked, Maddison told him about their confrontation in the alley. "He told Donovan his intervention with the contract was a favour, one he owed D's father. I didn't buy the story, but I believe he knows something."

"I don't like it. Not his new obsession with you-" Kian held up a hand when Maddison opened her mouth. "Zac told me about his visits, and when a god as powerful as Orion decides to get in your way, you need to be prepared." He paused outside the receiving room. "I'll reach out to the elders, find out what they know. In the meantime, I want you to be careful."

"If he wanted me dead he'd have left me at Firmani."

Kian gripped her gently by the shoulders. "Have you considered that he was the one who shot you in the first place?"

"For what purpose?" Maddison thought back to the attack, the burst of light she'd seen in her peripheral vision a second before the arrow struck, and her stomach dropped. "Was all this about loyalty? Do you think he wants me indebted to him?"

"I don't know. But I'm going to find out."

Maddison felt anger surge in her blood. She tamped it down, snuffed it out before she followed Kian into the room. Life sprang from the space; a group so animated it was like being back at Merc Hall. Kian had a large, extended family. The Gillifords always gathered at meal time. It was a happy home. Her gaze locked on Michael, who stopped arguing with his cousin to stare open-mouthed at her.

"What?" Maddison feigned innocence. "Do I have something on my face?"

Michael let out a whoop and bounded out of his chair. She met him at the top of the table, forgoing the usual elfin greeting to throw her arms around him. Only when they had hugged out the surge of emotion did Maddison drop back so he could rest his forehead against hers.

The room exploded as everybody began talking at once. Maddison was soon swept up in the drama. Here she could let down her guard, allow the feel of home to seep into her bones. Orion had to know that. Had he been assuaging his guilt for using her as a pawn?

You don't know for sure he fired the shot.

It seemed too extreme, even for Orion, who enjoyed to play his little games. The doubts niggled at her, prevented her from truly relaxing into her role within the family. Not that anyone but Kian suspected where her thoughts were.

An hour later, refuelled and fully healed, she returned to Michael's room to shower. Alone again, the scene at Firmani began playing on a loop. Maddison could think of no plausible reason that Orion would first shoot, and then save her life.

'Hey, half-blood. Do you have a sec?' It occurred to her, as she reached for the connection to Tobias in her mind, that she should reassure the others.

'I take it this means you won the battle?' His voice held a hint of amusement; a distinctive pattern in her head.

'This round at least. How are things going your end?' They had to be at Kevlar Wood by now.

'We hit a little trouble at Orca, and judging from Obadiah's interaction with Moi, the Alliance know he's here.'

Maddison felt her stomach sink. *'Obadiah was only in this region because of me, or should I say a particular god who enjoys to use me like a puppet.'*

'What's going on, Watcher?' The arrogance in his question made her smile; it was the voice of a king.

'I think I was targeted specifically. That my injury and the events which followed are all part of some crazy plan Orion is scheming up.' Maddison dropped onto the edge of the bed. *'There's nothing I can do about it now, and I'd like to return to my job. How accommodating is Sebastian feeling? I could use a lift.'*

Tobias' laughter rang in her head, soothing the anger and the tension. *'You make him sound like a taxi. I think Donovan is spoiling you.'*

Donovan, like all hympes, could transform into anything he desired. As part of the contract, he was supposed to spend prolonged periods of time bound to one shape, but Maddison had always played things fast and loose with the rules. When she needed transportation, Donovan enjoyed surprising her with a stream of vehicles so she could travel in style. Sebastian, on the other hand, being a member of the Fallen, could teleport to a given location.

'How is D?'

This time Tobias' mental voice held a note of pride. *'Doing a kick-ass job. He...'* Maddison's brow puckered at the prolonged silence. *'I'll fill you in later. I have to go.'*

Maddison wanted to tell him to be careful, but she knew he would not appreciate the sentiment. Besides, he had his guards to watch his back.

She was strapping on her boots when Kian entered with Michael. Kian looked incredibly pleased with himself, which meant he came bearing gifts. Maddison grinned when she saw the box in his hand – this should be good.

"I've been working on this for a while." Kian handed her the box; the weight took her by surprise. "It's similar to the capes the elders use, adapted to meet your particular needs."

Maddison dropped the box on the bed, feeling her stomach bounce like the mattress. Her hands shook as she removed the lid.

"Oh!" Her mouth fell open in appreciation. "Kian, it's magnificent."

She pulled the coat from the box. It was fashioned from the hide of a brascilloe; a sacred beast found only in elven territory. Brascilloes were marvellous creatures. They had a thick layer of protective skin, a layer they shed annually in a constant cycle of regrowth. The elves used these layers within enchantments, for decoration, or for protection; it was a highly respected tradition.

The coat was the darkest shade of green Maddison had come across, though brascilloes often changed their skin colour to suit the environment. It hummed with contained power, as though impatient to be worn. Maddison didn't need to be prompted again. She pushed her arms inside the sleeves and shrugged the material into place. It was a perfect fit; long and practical, it reached the heel of her boots.

"You made me a coat of invisibility." Her gaze locked with Kian. "That's what you meant about it being modelled from the capes, right?"

Kian nodded, his eyes aglow with pleasure. "It has another use too. I think you'll like it."

Michael's eye roll was exaggerated. He stepped past his father and came to a stop in front of her. "Seriously? You two get way too excited about this stuff." He ran a finger beneath the collar of the coat. "There's a spell woven into the seam here. If you activate it, the hood will unfold and the coat will work its magic. You'll be invisible." Michael looked down at her feet. "There's just one catch. You'll have to lose the boots."

Not a chance.

Her boots were as much a part of her as the suit she always wore. Maddison tested the pliability of the material, and was pleased by the give. "I'll crouch!"

Kian threw back his head and laughed; a booming sound which echoed around them. "Put her out of her misery, son, and show her what else the coat can do."

Michael obliged with a huge grin. He bent to gather the ends of the coat, pulling the material to the front so she could see the seam running down the centre of her back. With a tug the material tore in half. Maddison felt it stop just below her shoulder blades.

"Now spin," Michael said, stepping back.

Maddison turned, squealing with delight when the two halves fanned out; the motion creating serpent-like whips to stun her opponents in a fight.

"Father thought it would make a nice addition to the hair. When you stop spinning, the seam will knit itself back together."

She slowed her momentum, testing out the new addition to what was quickly becoming her elfin wardrobe. "I love it." She bowed. "Thank you, father."

Michael stepped to her. "We need to make a few adjustments. You won't be able to wear the sword you favour." He showed her the lining, and the pockets he had designed to house some of her weapons.

"You spoil me. Really." She gave him a quick hug. "Will you walk me out? I should really make my way to the others. I'm already a day behind."

"Of course. Come." He took her hand.

Maddison paused before Kian, tilting her head so he could rest his brow against hers. "Thank you."

"Any time, daughter. I'll contact you when I've spoken to the elders." He lifted his head so she could see his lopsided grin. "I've become somewhat accustomed to the telephone."

The thought always made Maddison laugh, and yet it was definitely better than astral projection. Not as tiring either.

"How are you feeling?" Michael asked, as they made their way down the hallway.

Juiced.

"Good. I feel good. Stop worrying about me."

He had a crease down the centre of his forehead; a dead giveaway. "Not much chance of that." Michael nudged her with his elbow. "Come visit when you win the round. And bring Zac with you."

"Deal."

When they reached the door Michael held up his palm, waiting until she placed her own against it. "Be well, sister."

"Stay safe, brother."

With a wink, by now part of their tradition, Maddison pushed her way outside.

TWELVE

Obadiah had almost forgotten how simple it could be to spend time with Zara. He had so many memories, some which sustained him, others which only served to torture. Yet, the journeys they had once taken together, the simple pleasure of her company, those were some of the best he had.

As they waited in line to step through the portal, Obadiah felt a stirring he couldn't identify. They had met surprisingly little resistance so far, despite their earlier detour. He could almost believe Aretha was granting them safe passage across the realm. But the Aretha he knew was not so accommodating. She had followed their progress, of that he had no doubt. Aretha knew everything that occurred, was powerful enough to detect his presence the moment he arrived.

Obadiah glanced across at Zara. He wasn't fooled by the deceptive lack of concern in her pretty face. She was aware of the potential threat in front of them; Obadiah knew how her mind worked.

"What is it?" he asked, when a frown formed between her eyebrows.

"Gregory…my sister is concerned for his safety." Her eyes met his. They were brimming with worry for her Ward. "Sebastian will wait until he knows we're safely in Aretha's territory and then assist however he can."

It was so natural to take her hand in his. "He'll be okay, Zara. As soon as we've warned Aretha of what's coming I'll take you to him."

Zara dropped her head, silent for a few moments as she gathered herself. "It's because we're close isn't it? Gregory is somehow part of this."

He couldn't lie, not when she was in so much pain. "Yes, and I promise I'll tell you everything I can. But first things first."

"First things first." Zara lifted her head, tilted it to nod at Donovan as they approached the portal.

Obadiah felt her tense as they stepped beneath the simple sign. Camouflaged as it was beneath ample vegetation, it nevertheless served as a reminder that the sorcerer who created the gateway had a twisted sense of humour.

They emerged on the other side, where the sheer beauty of Aretha Falls overshadowed everything above and below. Donovan let out a low whistle, his head tipped back as he stared at the monstrous mountain that was home to the fae queen.

The others were nowhere to be found, like they'd gotten off at the wrong stop, or been swallowed up by the mountain itself.

Obadiah could feel the protection barrier like a pulse along his skin. It would hurt a little, pushing through it. He didn't know how he knew that. But he did.

"Do you feel that?" Donovan said, turning to look at Zara.

At first Obadiah thought he was referring to Aretha's spell of protection. A second later he felt it too. A tension which vibrated along his nerve endings.

"Oh!" Zara's voice was soft, affectionate. Her attention was on the forest to their left.

Obadiah followed her gaze, noting the deep shadows. He spotted the big cat a second before Donovan did. The cat stalked closer, its shaggy mane identifying it as a member of the Panthera family.

Before Obadiah realised what was happening, Zara burst across the clearing. She threw her arms around the cat's neck and laughed in delight. To Obadiah's surprise, the cat made a sound so close to a purr he might as well have been a damned kitten.

Donovan glanced across at him with a puzzled expression, stepping forward as Obadiah did to join Zara and her new friend.

"Fitz, it's so good to see you," Zara said, stroking a hand down the cat's back in a way Obadiah immediately envied.

The growl became a rumbling laugh as Fitz changed into his human form and threw his arms around her. Envy ramped up to pure jealousy, until Obadiah could barely see straight. "I take it you two know each other." He flicked his wrist, and clothed Fitz in a pair of shorts.

"Thanks, man." Fitz grinned as he glanced down.

"Fitz is a friend of Zachariah's," Zara explained, doing her best to hide the smile.

A vampire and a changeling, he found that very hard to believe. But he didn't say so. "It's good to meet you. I assume you're one of Aretha's scouts?"

The feline smile grew on Fitz's face. "She's waiting for you. Your friends joined the after-party; there was quite a brawl."

"You intercepted the welcoming committee." There was a hint of concern in Zara's voice, though Obadiah couldn't pinpoint the root of it.

Fitz shrugged. "They left us no choice. We're in a mating cycle so emotions are running high." Fitz glanced at Donovan. "I'll take you to the others. We'll be breaking things up shortly and heading out. Otherwise, things will get pretty intense around here." He winked at Zara.

Obadiah wanted to punch him in the face, which was such a human response he almost laughed at himself. Then again, Obadiah rarely took an instant disliking to another being, but the cat grated along his nerves.

"It was good to meet you," Obadiah said, his voice as dismissive as his words.

Fitz bowed his head, before dropping a kiss on Zara's cheek and blending back into the shadows. A second later, his voice drifted towards them. "You coming?"

"It's okay, Donovan." Zara put a hand on his arm. "We're safe where we're going."

Donovan nodded once, and then followed the cat into the dark.

After a beat or two of silence, Zara turned away. "Sebastian and Zachariah just left to check on Gregory. They'll be here by the time we get back."

Obadiah glanced toward the forest, wondering at the group beyond the trees. He could feel them, knew his team were safe, relieved they had arrived at their destination.

"Why do you look so worried?" Zara asked as they stepped toward the mountain.

He shrugged. "The last time I saw Aretha things didn't go well, and now I'm…" He waved a hand in front of his body. "Restricted."

"You put those restrictions on yourself." Zara's eyes flashed. "How do you know what you're capable of as a human if you keep the core of yourself locked inside?"

I'll never know what it is to be human.

"This body can't handle my power." He paused when he felt the barrier. It called to him, a clear indication Aretha was growing impatient. He turned to nod at Zara. "Let's get this over with."

They crossed through the barrier together, and crumpled to the floor at almost the same instant. The pain cut him off at the knees, blew his shields apart like so much glass; shards which buried themselves in Zara.

She was panting softly beside him, her face aglow with shocked understanding.

Crap.

Slowly the pain began to fade, until Obadiah could all but feel his barriers sliding back into place. Except it was too late. Zara knew.

Obadiah blinked his eyes to clear them, his mind whirring as it flicked through possible scenarios. Lying wasn't an option, so they had to deal with the emotional storm swirling around them before they faced Aretha.

He turned to Zara, took in her laboured breathing and pained expression. "Can you stand?"

When she didn't respond, he stood and bent to scoop her into his arms. He carried her to a cave opening, an entrance which hadn't been there a moment ago; stepping into the darkness with a sense of dread.

***

Zara fought to concentrate, to stay in the present, but the memories tore through her brain and dragged her back under. The pain was intense, a shard of emotion which pierced with every new memory, every new scene. She grabbed hold of one, hoping to slow the barrage, and was thrown into a nightmare.

It was a battlefield. The smell of burning flesh and freshly spilled blood wound its way around her, competing with the crippling agony of so much raw emotion. Her gaze scanned those still standing; a group of demons she recognised as Tuxaponz. They were horned beasts, their bulk intimidating; their blood hunger terrifying.

Zara's blood ran ice cold when she spotted Obadiah in the middle of the group. He had a gash along his cheek, and another across the long line of his jaw. He looked different, and for a moment she didn't understand why. And then it came to her. This was the real Obadiah, unhindered by a human vessel.

Her vision wavered as her mind tried to make sense of past and present. She wasn't really here, and Obadiah wasn't in any danger. Still, she couldn't take her eyes from the image he presented. He was tall, and long-limbed. His sandy hair shone like a beacon against their dark surroundings. She couldn't see them, but she knew his eyes were a startling aquamarine.

Zara's eyes followed his movements, watched as he raised his arms, and brought his hands together in a resounding snap. The shock wave lifted the Tuxamponz off their feet, slamming them back to the ground with enough force to render them immobile.

'Zara. Can you hear me?'

That voice. So familiar, so proud. It was a sound she heard in her head as often as her own thoughts.

'Zara?'

She heard the thunderous sound again, and blinked to refocus her mind. When her vision cleared, instead of the battleground, she saw Obadiah in his human form. He had brought her back to the present.

"I don't understand." The pain of knowing he had been taken from her was greater than anything she had experienced in her long, long life. "Why were the memories hidden from me?"

Obadiah closed his eyes as if he too was consumed by sorrow. "We were punished for breaking the rules."

The memories were a jumbled mess. Zara didn't have the strength to look at them too closely for fear they would drag her under. It hurt that she was capable of forgetting him. She had such love in her heart. How could it all just disappear?

There has always been something missing.

"When did your memories return?" A shiver ran through her when he didn't answer. "Obadiah. Talk to me." Zara placed her hand on his cheek. "And stop hiding your emotions. You don't need to do that anymore."

Obadiah opened his eyes; so dark they were almost black. "Trust me. I do." He sat back and gave her room to look around.

They were in a small cavern; a chamber of sorts. Zara had no idea where the light was coming from; it appeared to shine through the surface of the stone. A luminescent mineral perhaps.

"I was always meant to be a Prime."

She glanced back at him, saw that his eyes held more shadows than their surroundings. "I know. You were born into the role. It's your destiny." Zara frowned, alarmed by the words. At the knowledge behind them. Her eyes never left Obadiah's, but her mind was sifting through the information. It came to her in snippets of memory. The fact it had been part of his initiation to train with the Guardians, and the reason they met. No, that wasn't quite right.

Zara smiled when the detail fell into place. They weren't part of the same unit, but they had been drawn to each other. Even then.

The three of us.

"Jeremiah." Zara felt a fresh wave of pain stab her heart. "They took him from me too." They were family. What could they have possibly done to deserve the severity of their punishment?

"We screwed up," Obadiah said, reading her thoughts.

Zara crawled over to him. She needed to be near him, to use his strength. Wasn't that what they had always done? Supported one another. "I need to see. Help me remember."

Obadiah touched his fingers to her forehead, creating a link between them. Zara saw a young woman in her mind, as clear as if she were sitting beside them.

They had been sent on a mission, a mission to help this poor soul who walked a dangerous path. Zara felt the echo of her pain, remembered how it had felt to be in the room with her; trapped with the anger and sorrow.

It had been worse for Jeremiah. Their friend had formed an instant bond with the girl, and though he blasted her with wave after wave of light and affection, he couldn't save her. She would have overdosed, had chosen to return home, but Jeremiah intervened. He broke his vows by trying to stop her, regardless of her choice.

"He was trying to save her." Zara's voice was a whisper. "Why were we punished because he loved her too much?"

"You know why. There are rules, and we broke them. I could have stopped him. We both knew he was in too deep, and yet we did nothing."

"So they wiped our memories?"

Obadiah dropped his hand, "I should be so lucky." He stood so she couldn't see his face, pacing the small space. "Jeremiah was stripped of his rank and sent to the human realm to live out his penance."

Zara stood too, her mind reeling with shock. She understood the penalties for disobedience, but rarely were they so extreme. "Why didn't we share the same fate?" she asked, feeling nauseous again.

"I told you. I was destined to be a Prime, so they couldn't strip my status."

Obadiah had his back to her, the lines of his shoulders so tense she knew he was fighting to keep his emotions in check. "You spoke up for me, didn't you?"

"I did what I could to lighten your sentence. Jeremiah's, too. The Alliance agreed to wipe your memory and allow you to keep your status as a Guardian." He finally turned to her. "The only thing they took from you was us."

She felt no bitterness from him, only loss, and it lanced through her heart. "And you?"

"Me? I got to keep my memories and lost you anyway."

The injustice of it brought tears to her eyes. "I'm so sorry." Zara stepped forward to wrap her arms around him. She laid her head against his heart, humbled by his strength. They had been more than friends, more than lovers, they were two parts of a whole.

Obadiah stood rigid; his body as hard as the cavern walls. Zara held on patiently, inhaling a rush of breath when his arms came around her.

"There's more," he said after a few minutes. "The connection you feel to Gregory, the reason you-"

Zara gasped and stepped back so she could see his face. "He's Jeremiah."

"Yes."

Her mind whirled. It made perfect sense now; her desperation to save him. The kinship. Everything.

"They're using his blood against us." Zara's felt a wave of nausea. "How did they find out who he is?"

Obadiah shook his head. "I don't know. But it's not a secret, the fact there are exiled Guardians within the mortal realm. Draco has powerful friends."

"We need to warn him. We have to tell-"

Obadiah put a finger against her lips, silencing her. "Sebastian and Zachariah can handle it." His look turned sheepish. "And I told Lucas what I know. He won't allow Draco to harm him."

"I still need to see him." Zara buried her head against his chest again, her mind racing. "Did we stand like this, before they took my memories? Did they let us say goodbye?"

"No." A wave of anger hit her as Obadiah let go of the leash. He was remembering their last moments together.

"I'm sorry for that too." She didn't want to think about how much harder it would be this time. Now she knew the truth, she understood they were on borrowed time.

Obadiah kissed the top of her head, smoothing her hair in a way both familiar and new. "We should go. Aretha is not known for her patience." When Zara stepped back, Obadiah took her hand.

The tunnel was narrow in places, with jagged rock and wide, gaping crevices she suspected housed a variety of cave-dwelling species. She concentrated on that until she was sure she was fully rooted in the here and now. Finally, when she'd begun to suspect the tunnel led into the very Abyss itself, it opened up. They were close.

THIRTEEN

They were silent as they journeyed beneath the last stretch of mountain. Obadiah knew something had changed between them, and he was almost sorry he'd held back. But he couldn't tell her he had tortured himself for hundreds of years as he watched her; couldn't afford to let her see into his heart. It would destroy them both.

Their time was limited, there was nothing he could do about that. But he could protect her.

Obadiah knew what was waiting for them beyond the exit, and he was glad he could give Zara the experience.

It was clear, given the lack of interference by the Alliance, that Aretha was curious enough to assert her influence over the council. The Fae Queen was a force to be reckoned with; she expected allegiance. Rarely did the elders deny her anything. She had been granted her own realm, was allowed to rule as she chose; a testament to the power she possessed. Obadiah had been raised on the stories of Aretha's glory. It was said she was born from the true light, that she was a fragment of the heart, set free to live as one with the darkness.

"I can feel the magic," Zara said, distracting him from his thoughts.

"Some would say it's an aphrodisiac," he said, and smiled as they emerged into the light.

Aretha Falls was set in a valley between two mountains. The cave ended in the centre of one of those mountains; one of the only access points.

The ledge where they stood was an enchanted bridge suspended three thousand feet from the ground, providing a view of the Falls. It was breathtaking; a mixture of nature and enchantment.

A shelf directly beneath them jutted out of the mountain and wound itself in graceful arcs, round and round until it reached the floor. Each layer was resplendent with trees of so many varieties it was impossible to tell them apart. Homes were dotted throughout, houses which were so clearly part of the tree it might have grown that way.

A thundering waterfall dropped over the side of the mountain, the water feeding an invisible slipstream which provided nutrients to the land. To the naked eye the water was swallowed by the ground, soaking the earth in perpetual growth.

Zara looked over the railing. "How do we get down?" He could hear the wonder in her voice, understood the power of the place.

The kingdom below was dominated by a structure carved from the rock itself. It was a vision of smooth rock face, a translucent colour that shone like glass. The water cast a mysterious glow along the structure as though it were being absorbed and used as an energy source. Thousands of orbs, in a rainbow of startling colour, lit the scene.

"We wait." Obadiah smiled, his head tilted up; searching the skies.

A large, fiery red dragon appeared, hovering before them with what Obadiah recognised as an arrogant smile.

Its long, surprisingly smooth tail, curled toward them. Obadiah grabbed Zara's hand and hopped on, walking the unusual path to the centre of the dragon's back. Here they settled themselves, clinging tightly to some of the larger scales so they didn't plummet to the ground below.

'This is Aretha, isn't it?' The shock was evident in Zara's mental voice.

"The original shape-shifter," he said, speaking aloud because he knew Aretha heard everything. "Many species evolved from the faery."

"I know that, genius." She had remembered something else. Obadiah was sure of it. He'd heard those words so many times it took him back too, to their early days in the Academy.

The memory drifted away out of reach, the instant they made it to the ground. In a flash of scarlet, Aretha transformed into her human form. Her waves of fiery red hair spilled over her shoulders to taper at her slender waist.

"Obadiah." Aretha stepped forward to place a kiss on his forehead. "What a treat this is."

He looked up into shocking green eyes and wondered briefly if she shared a genetic link to Maddison; he hadn't thought of it until now, but their eyes were almost identical.

He bowed. "Thank you for our safe passage."

Aretha was already moving to Zara. She took both her hands, her smile resplendent. "It's a pleasure to finally meet you, Zara the Fair."

"The pleasure is mine." Zara bent to touch her head to their joined hands.

"I assume the circumstances warrant the risks you've taken," Aretha said, turning back to Obadiah.

"Have you ever known me to act impulsively?" He laughed at her raised brows. Aretha had always appreciated the direct approach. "I came because you're in danger. Draco seeks entry into your realm and plans to use the Fallen to do it."

Aretha showed no outward reaction to the news. "Come. Let's walk."

They followed her, Zara struggling to match her long strides as she cut across to a garden of pretty wild flowers.

"He seeks the Band of Ubiquity, I presume." Aretha glanced briefly at Zara. "Which means he found a way to control the Fallen."

"He has the blood of an outcast, and he's using it to create an army." Obadiah recognised the impatience in her expression, and hurried on. "We know he's gaining in power. He may already have what he needs to enter the Falls, so we ask for your assistance." He bowed again, wishing he could read her thoughts.

Aretha ran her fingertips across a pretty white blossom, her face pensive. "I've been meaning to take a vacation." Her laughing eyes met his. "I will protect my people, and secure the key. But I cannot directly intervene unless Draco moves against me."

"How may we assist?" Zara's eyes were downcast. "There has to be something we can do."

"You need to destroy the remaining vials of blood." Aretha stretched out her long, elegant fingers and removed a ruby ring. "Ensure the outcast is wearing this before they drain him completely. It will bind him to me."

"Which means he'll be under your protection." It was a clever move. If the Fractured attempted to harm Jeremiah, Aretha would destroy them. "What of the Alliance? They have special interest in him too."

"Are you doubting my power?"

Obadiah looked into eyes of enchanting green, and shivered against the cold light of their disapproval. "Forgive me, I meant no offence. We will ensure Jeremiah receives the gift." He reached out to take the ring, flinching when her hand wrapped tightly around his.

"Pray you're not too late, Wanderer. This is a battle you can't afford to lose. Not if you want to win the war." Aretha released his hand with a small smile. "But now, as you've come so far, we shall have tea."

"Thank you for your hospitality." Obadiah managed to keep the impatience from his tone. He had to tread carefully. Aretha could crush him like a bug in this form.

Aretha started to turn and stopped, glancing at him with amusement. "You can tell your friends they are free to leave."

As they followed Aretha down the flower strewn path, Obadiah took Zara's hand in his. He gave it a gentle squeeze before releasing her. It irked him they had to play such games, that their journey had been necessary due to the limits on his power. But, of course, Aretha would allow them to travel through her shields. They had earned that right.

'Your Highness.' Obadiah's thoughts reached easily through the barrier to brush against Tobais' mind. *'Aretha will allow us safe passage from her realm. Thank you for your assistance.'*

'Of course she will.' He could hear the smile in the king's voice. *'Is the dragon putting you through your paces?'*

Obadiah heard Aretha's muffled laughter ahead of him, and knew she was listening in on their conversation.

'You spend too much time with Maddison.' Tobias' amusement rang in his head for a moment. *'Her majesty is a gracious host. We're having tea.'*

After a beat or two of silence, laughter sounded again. *'Which means she's listening. No offence, Aretha, but you can be one scary bitch.'*

Obadiah groaned, drawing Zara's attention. He tapped his head. "Tobias has been taking lessons from your witch. He has no respect for authority."

Zara smiled, and gave a brief shrug. "Tobias doesn't need any lessons, but he's the most respectful being I know. Which is why Aretha is amused by his teasing."

Zara was right, of course. As Obadiah watched, Aretha's whole body language changed. She was enjoying herself.

He shrugged, tuning out the conversation in his head, just as Tobias was pledging his allegiance. In a roundabout way.

***

Tobias laughed as Aretha's voice faded from his mind. She was a fair and generous ruler, and for that fact alone she had his loyalty.

"Sire?" Marcus was watching him with a curious expression.

"Just a little flirtation between king and queen." Tobias grinned at his second in command. "We've been given the okay to leave. You can tell the others."

"Did you tell them she's on her way?" Marcus gave him a knowing look. "Maddison will be pissed that she arrived a day late to the party."

The twins had spotted Maddison twenty minutes ago, which meant she would reach them within another five; judging by the speed she was moving. "Don't be getting any ideas." Tobias narrowed his eyes in warning. "She'll be looking for a fight and you're easy pickings."

That warranted a nasty grin from Marcus. "The cats cheated us all. Maddison isn't the only one looking for a little payback."

"We need to conserve our energy. This isn't over."

With a nod, Marcus walked toward the group gathered by an impromptu camp. Less than a minute later they were headed back to the Orcas. Donovan and Riley walked slightly ahead, clearly hoping to intercept their friend.

They didn't have to wait long. Tobias spotted her immediately. She was back in the suit, though she had a new addition to her wardrobe. The long, dark coat swung as she walked, and Tobias' heart sped up. Maddison could be intimidating under normal circumstances, now she looked dangerous and as sexy as hell.

'Nice coat.' Tobias' mental voice betrayed his reaction to her.

Maddison met his gaze before turning to Donovan who had stepped in her path. "I'm okay, D." Her expression softened, and Tobias wondered what Donovan had said to her.

Whatever it was, she clamped a hand on his shoulder. The 'oof' was silent as Donovan threw his arms around her. She hesitated for only a second and then hugged him back.

After a tense silence, Donovan finally released her. "You scared the hell out of me."

Tobias could sympathise. He'd been terrified. He didn't hear what she said, something sardonic judging by Donovan's bark of laughter.

He was about to step forward when Riley stole his thunder, his big body vibrating with tension as he stood shoulder to shoulder with Donovan.

"Now don't go soft on me, wolf-man." Maddison narrowed her eyes, assessing him. "I've been injured worse than that in the dining hall." She placed a palm over Riley's heart in that way she had of soothing his beast. "You don't get rid of me that easily."

Riley's grunt had a surprised sound to it, probably due to the fact Sebastian appeared on Maddison's left without warning.

"Good to see you up and about," Sebastian said, giving her a once over. "Nice coat."

"If we had time I'd give you a demonstration." Maddison rolled her eyes. "What happened?"

"We had to move Zara's Ward, and we need to secure the property." Sebastian glanced at Donovan and Riley. "The more the merrier."

'Zara's safe.' Tobias caught the lick of confusion on Maddison's face and knew it would annoy her she was out of the loop. He stepped forward at last, meeting Sebastian's expression. "Can you take the others first. I want a moment alone with Maddison."

As though to demonstrate how little time he had, or patience, Sebastian put a hand on Riley and Donovan and disappeared with a nod.

'Give us a minute.' Tobias instructed Marcus, but his second was already making himself scarce, taking the other hunters with him.

"What is wrong with everybody?" Maddison snapped, walking to meet him. "We all get injured. It goes with the territory."

Tobias reached out a hand, amused when her braid whipped out to snag his wrist. It was such a relief to realise she was back to full strength it made his head spin. "You were out for a long time. We're not used to that." He took a step closer and she didn't protest. The soft strands of her hair didn't tighten in warning as he'd expected.

There was barely an inch between them now. "Don't say no." Tobias waited, searching her face for any clue of what she was feeling.

"I don't have all-"

He silenced her words with a kiss, ready for the emotion which flooded his body whenever he touched her.

Maddison released his wrist, grabbing a handful of his shirt to pull him closer. She returned the kiss, unleashing the passion he recognised at his very core. But there was something different about her taste, about the power he felt humming along her skin.

He stepped back so he could see her eyes. "How did you return to full strength so quickly?"

"I have friends in high places." Maddison winked at him, stepping back. "Do you have it out of your system now, this…" she waved a hand toward him. "Whatever it is?"

"Not even close." Tobias smiled when she narrowed her eyes, wishing he had more time. "If Obadiah decides to make a move against Draco I want in."

Maddison glanced over his shoulder and he knew Sebastian had arrived. "Deal. We'll need all the help we can get." She stepped around him. "Catch you later, half-blood."

She was gone before he had time to reply. *'Try to avoid any more arrows.'*

The sound of Maddison's laughter in his head, soothed the remnants of doubt about her condition. However she'd won the internal battle, she was back, and more than capable of taking care of herself.

FOURTEEN

Zachariah was waiting when they arrived at the safe house. Sebastian inclined his head in greeting, before jogging up the steps to the old farmhouse.

"Where are we?" Maddison turned in a circle, taking in the copse of trees which surrounded the property. Definitely in the country, somewhere relatively untouched by the war.

Zachariah shrugged. "Somewhere in Hampshire." When she moved to stand beside him, facing the steps, he nudged her with his shoulder. "Good to have you back."

"Don't tell me you want a hug too?" Maddison laughed when he raised one eyebrow, Marcus wasn't the only one who watched too much television.

"I'm okay, but thanks." He nudged her again.

As they walked up the steps, Maddison took in the neat lines of the building; relieved there was only one exit to defend. "Michael wants us to visit when this is all over."

Zachariah paused by the door. "I have something to take care of first, but I'll make a visit."

She reached to cover his hand with hers. "I know my timing isn't great, but you need to talk to me, Zac. I can't help you if you shut me out."

"You're right. Your timing sucks." Zachariah turned to meet her gaze. He smiled to lighten the blow. "When we get through this I'll tell you everything."

"Maybe a hint?" Maddison was teasing, but it wasn't until his face fell that she understood how bad it was.

"Jax is missing." Zachariah closed his eyes. "He's disappeared before, but this time it's different."

Jax was Zachariah's feeding partner. Vampires were the offspring of the Enraptured and a species of Clanderian known as the Lechen tribe. They needed blood to survive, and the only source containing the sustenance they required was the blood of a Clanderian. The two races formed a tentative alliance, providing the other with feeding partners as a way to continue the bloodline.

"How long before I should start to worry?"

Zachariah rolled his eyes. "Contrary to popular belief, you worry too much." He turned the doorknob. "Let's deal with one thing at a time. I'm not going to start snacking on the blood of the innocent."

"Yes, because that's what I'm worried about. You-" Maddison clamped her mouth shut when it registered they weren't alone. The small foyer was crowded, in fact, and all eyes were on them.

"You must be feeling better if you're already giving Zac a hard time." Zara's face relaxed into a smile. "Thanks for letting me know you were okay, by the way."

Maddison pulled a face. "I sent instructions with Michael, which could be classed as giving you a hard time, and based on your diagnosis that should tell you-"

"That you're a pain in my ass even as you sleep." Zara held up her hand so Maddison could slap their palms together; a customary high-five.

"So who's going to bring me up to speed?" It was almost comical, the way they glanced at one another; they were practically squirming. It told her she wasn't going to like it. "Spill."

Obadiah stepped forward. He held his hand up, palm facing her. "May I? It would save some time."

Something had changed, something significant. "Okay."

Obadiah moved his hand so it rested just above her head. "Close your eyes."

She did as he asked, flinching when she felt the connection. And then she lived the last day in reverse, through Obadiah's eyes; the scenes and images flickering so bright and fast she couldn't keep up.

It hurt her head and, strangely, her heart, so she was glad when he moved back. The movie playing in her head snapped off, leaving a hum of tension behind.

"Excuse us." Maddison took Zara's hand and dragged her out of the foyer into a hall. When they were out of ear shot she rounded on her. "What the hell?"

"Don't give me that look. I'm not going to call Lucas, or inform the Alliance. I won't put Obadiah and Gregory at risk." Zara stared back at her, her face mutinous.

"But he's not a mortal boy named Gregory, is he? His name is Jeremiah and protecting each other is what got you into this mess in the first place." Maddison paced in a tight circle, trying and failing to find her calm.

"And you wouldn't do the same if this was about Michael and Zachariah?" Zara held up a hand. "It doesn't matter, because this is about preventing Draco from getting his hands on the key, so we have more important things to worry about."

Maddison felt her anger ignite, and she had to clamp down on her impulses because Zara was close to the edge too. "More important than protecting people? How can you protect those in your care if they strip you of your status?"

"I'm protecting Obadiah. Somebody has to. Think about it, Maddy." Zara put a hand on her shoulder to stop the angry pacing. "He thinks I don't know he's been looking out for me all these years, centuries of self-induced torture. Think about what that must be like, the pain it had to cause him. I didn't even remember him and yet he sacrificed everything anyway."

Crap. Crap. Crap.

Zara was right. Obadiah had risked his life to warn them of the coming battle, regardless of his true motivation. He shouldn't be punished for loving Zara that much.

"It's my job to protect you. If I don't report this, then even if you're not punished, I will be. I'll be removed from the Legion. How will I do my job then?"

How will I help you to pick up the pieces when Obadiah is gone?

"You've always followed your own rules, Maddy. It's why the Alliance chose you, even if they would never admit it." Zara squeezed her shoulder. "And I might be your Charge, but I'm also your friend." Her smile was gentle. "Which is what this is really about."

Maddison rolled her eyes. "Just think about what's at stake, okay. There are too many variables and I don't like it."

"Duly noted." Zara glanced to the ceiling. "But right now, there's a young boy upstairs who needs me. He might have the soul of a Guardian, but he doesn't know it. He's frightened."

"Okay. You deal with Jeremiah, and I'll prepare the ingredients. If we have to destroy the remaining vials in Draco's possession, we're going to need a location spell." Maddison blew out a breath. "And I'm going to need more of Jeremiah's blood."

"I'll take care of it."

"You do that." Maddison did a quick survey of the room. "I'm going to take a look around this place, and get a lay of the land. I don't like surprises, and there have been far too many." She turned toward a flight of stairs without waiting for Zara's response.

***

The foyer was empty when Zara returned. She walked through into the small receiving room on the left and found Obadiah looking out of a large, picture-frame window.

He turned when she entered. "How fairs your witch?"

"Why do you call her that – my witch?" Zara walked to a high-backed chair and lowered herself into it. She was exhausted.

"It's the truth. We are nothing without connection, you once told me that. The ties which bind you to Maddison are strong." Obadiah walked toward her. "There is more than one kind of soul mate."

Zara nodded. "There's one upstairs right now and he needs me." She smiled. "He needs you too, though he doesn't know it."

"Then go to him and wake Jeremiah."

She closed her eyes, gathering her energy into a tight ball. After a moment she stepped out of her human body, like it was nothing more than a work suit.

"Zara." Obadiah's voice with husky with emotion.

"I know it's foolish. But I wanted to try connecting with him as I am, as the one he-"

Obadiah cupped her face, the feel of him different now, more intimate. "It's not foolish. But you need to go easy on him, Zara. He may not remember, you must accept that before you go in."

"I know." Zara blinked back her tears and hurried from the room. She didn't stop until she rounded a curve at the top of the stairs and caught her reflection in the antique mirror.

It wasn't the first time she'd looked upon her true from, and yet it felt like an eternity since she had felt this whole. Everything about her form was different to her human half. She was several inches taller, her hair darker, and eyes paler. But none of it mattered because at the heart of her, of all her kind, shone a light so bright, so distinct, it was the only truth. She just hoped Gregory recognised it.

It's Jeremiah.

She spotted Sebastian a moment later. "Zara." His face was twisted in concern. "Are you sure about this. It might help if Jerry made an appearance."

Was it a coincidence she had chosen that name as her alias, a variation of Jeremiah. Zara doubted it. "I have a feeling, Seb." She ran a hand down her brother's arm. "Trust me."

"Always." Sebastian inclined his head. "I'm here if you need me."

Zara walked to the door of Gregory's room. She could feel his fear, it drifted toward her like a dense fog. She had to put her hand against the frame to steady herself, which only made it worse. Gregory's thoughts came fast and furious, 'What were those things? Why was I taken? What's going to happen to me?' They were accompanied by the same four images; demons in human skin, an angel, a vampire, and a strange, old house he didn't recognise.

The angel and vampire would be hard enough to explain, even if they were her brother and his Watcher. The demons, what happened from here on out, those things were going to require a heavy dose of faith. The world knew demons were real, the war left few in doubt of their existence. So at least she didn't have to bring out the monster card.

The longer Zara stood, the more her doubt blossomed; fed by Gregory's. Blast after blast of fear and uncertainty hit her, until there was no choice but to raise her shields.

She opened the door cautiously, as though approaching a cornered animal. Gregory was sat on a large, double bed, his long, gangly limbs curled up into a tight ball.

His mouth dropped open when he saw her, his intense brown eyes full of surprise. "I know you."

"Do you?" Zara closed the door softly, afraid any sudden move would put him on edge.

"You're in my dreams." His eyes narrowed. "Are you a demon too?"

Zara's smile was ironic. "It depends who you ask. But no. I'm an angel, a fallen angel to be exact."

Lines appeared in Gregory's forehead as he processed that. "What do you want with me?"

"What I've always wanted. To protect you." She decided to stay where she was for the next part. "Don't be afraid, Gregory. I'm not going to hurt you, but this might make it easier to understand."

Zara applied the filter so, to Gregory, she now resembled his friend. The boy he had grown to trust since they had collided on his way home from school.

A squeak of surprise erupted from Gregory's throat, as a wave of emotion swamped the room.

"Jerry?" It was an accusation.

"It's what we call a filter, a form which is unique to each of our Wards." Zara dropped the mask. "Jerry is who you needed at the time."

"So you lied to me?" His voice held a bitter note she found preferable to his fear.

"I never lied to you, Gregory. I concealed my true identity because there was no other way to reach you. But I'm still your friend."

Gregory shook his head. "You could have tried."

"I did try."

The minutes ticked by as Gregory considered her words. Zara knew he was looking back on that time in his life, a time he so desperately needed a friend. "The Guidance Counsellor." Gregory tipped his head to the side. "You looked different then. Less like…"

"An angel?"

He shrugged, relaxing a little. "I guess it explains the dreams. I'd forgotten about Mrs Jenkins."

Zara trusted her instincts, and what his body language was telling her. She walked across to the bed. "There might be another reason for the dreams. Can you tell me about them?"

Gregory's face flushed, and for one horrible moment she didn't want to know.

"Mainly you're injured. I find you bleeding in the street and carry you to safety." He shrugged again, his face pink. "You usually tease me about coming to your rescue."

Zara sat on the edge of the bed, keeping as much distance between them as she could, so he didn't feel crowded. "What do you think the dreams mean?"

"That I've seen too much footage of the war and wanted to play hero."

She laughed, and was pleased when he grinned back at her. "You've never played at hero." She knew it was the wrong thing to say the instant his face fell. As usual, she was getting ahead of herself. "What I mean is. The dream is something else. It's a repressed memory."

Gregory frowned, his whole demeanour turning sceptical. "I don't know what you mean."

Think, Zara. Think.

"What do you know about angels?" she asked, settling on the truth, or building up to it at least.

"Other than the fact they play with people's minds? Not a lot."

Gregory had always been a bright child, and Zara knew his words were a test; to see whether he could anger her. What he didn't know, something which went soul deep, was that Jeremiah had always had a smart mouth. So the answer only made her smile.

"There are many species of angel. The ones you'll probably identify with are what mortals call guardian angels. But we'll come back to Guardians." Zara sat more comfortably on the mattress, crossing her legs. "There are also Warrior angels, those who defend the realms and are used in times of war, who are, incidentally, the only angels with wings."

"I've seen the footage." Gregory smiled, looking every bit the teenager. "They're kick ass."

"Indeed. And I guess the hierarchy isn't important right now, except to mention all angel kind are governed by the Primes. They-"

"Primes? Seriously?"

Please don't make a reference to pop culture.

Zara raised her eyebrows. "Moving on. There are rules we must follow, and if we break them there are consequences."

Gregory shifted on the bed. "Where are you going with this?"

"I started out as a Guardian, angels who serve and protect all souls on earth. During my training I met a fellow Guardian, Jeremiah, and we were instant friends. We trained together, sometimes fought together, and basically broke every rule in basic training." Zara paused to look at him.

"You're not telling me I've been possessed by an angel?"

She let out a frustrated breath. "Angels do not possess people. We use human hosts when we fall, but the soul has crossed over before…never mind." Zara ran a hand through her hair. "Jeremiah was punished for breaking the rules."

We were all punished.

"He was stripped of his status and cast out, to spend his sentence in the mortal realm."

Disbelief shadowed Gregory's eyes, an emotion which morphed into terror. Zara had no idea where the emotion had come from, and then she felt it. A threat she would have detected before it formed, if her energies weren't divided. She was vulnerable without her human shell, leaving herself open like this had been a mistake.

As Zara turned towards the growing portal at her back, Gregory dove on top of her. Whether an instinctive need to protect, she couldn't be sure. She didn't get the chance to find out. Two things happened simultaneously: the door to the room burst open and she was sucked into the portal with Gregory wrapped tightly around her. The last thing she saw before the bedroom disintegrated from view was Maddison making a leap toward her.

FIFTEEN

"NO!" Obadiah stormed into Jeremiah's room just as Maddison was hitting the carpet.

"Son of a bitch." She was on her feet a moment later, her long braid twitching with irritation. "No offence. But I think it's about time we called in the big guns."

Obadiah had a strong urge to hit something. All his plans and he had failed to achieve the most important one of all. Protecting Zara.

Maddison was watching him like a hawk; her instincts exceptional. "I'd gladly go a few rounds with you, angel-boy, but we don't have the time."

"It would be wise to remember who you're referring to, Watcher." He could tell she didn't like him using the name.

Her eyes flashed with green fire. "News flash. Down here we're the same. We're all fighting a war, and I don't have time for this bullshit."

Obadiah's left palm began to itch and, when he looked down, his hand was consumed in blue flame. He glanced back at Maddison. "You will show me some respect."

"Respect has to be earned, and right now-"

"Why don't you both take a step back," Donovan said, walking to stand shoulder to shoulder with Maddison; his loyalties clear. "You're both blaming yourselves and it won't get us anywhere."

Maddison held up her hands. "Okay fine. But we're going to need some help, that's all I'm saying. I don't have Gregory...Jeremiah...whoever. I don't have his blood, so I can't locate them."

Obadiah fingered the ring in his pocket. They hadn't given the object of protection to Jeremiah yet, either.

They all turned when Sebastian flashed into the room, his face pale and drawn. "I can't connect to her. I can always reach her. Always."

"Draco planned this, which means he thought of the basics. He's using a concealment spell." Maddison began to pace. "I assume you tried teleporting anyway?"

Sebastian didn't answer. He was already gone.

"If you're right, the port could have killed him." Obadiah resisted the urge to nail Maddison's feet to the carpet. She expelled so much energy it was exhausting to watch.

The fact was, Sebastian needed a link to port to a person; images only worked with a specific place. Trying to find Zara based on an image was futile, and dangerous. There were echoes of her throughout the Enchanted realm; Sebastian could have been playing directly into Draco's hands.

"She's his sister. He had to try." Maddison's face softened, just a fraction. "We'll find her. If-" She grinned at Sebastian's return. He'd brought a friend along. "Lucas. We could use a hand right about now."

Lucas raised his brows, humour tugging his lips. "Even I have my limits." He turned to meet Obadiah's gaze; never breaking eye contact, though he bowed his head. "Zara and Jeremiah are in the Realm of the Lost. I can get you in, but I can't pinpoint a location."

"Is it Jeremiah or Zara who tipped the scales?" Obadiah asked, not bothering to hide his bitterness. "Who warrants your assistance?"

Lucas' gaze was unwavering. "You make the rules, do you not? Why don't you tell me?"

"What's that supposed to mean?"

Obadiah ignored Maddison's question. If he truly made the rules he would have his full powers and Draco would not be permitted a freedom he did not deserve. "You don't want to push me right now, Luke. You're her friend and you did nothing to protect her from this."

"He did what he could." Sebastian stepped between them. "He spoke up for our family when the Fractured began targeting-"

"Will you please save this pissing contest for another time?" Maddison was glaring at them, her plait swishing like a cat's tail. "My Ward is in trouble, and right now it's the only thing I care about."

"She's right, of course." Lucas bowed more deeply this time. "And since Draco has the Book of Ignis there's no time to waste."

Obadiah felt a cold shiver scuttle across his soul. "He has what?"

"I assumed you knew." Lucas took a step back. "He needed it to complete the binding ritual."

Ignis was a goddess of fire; a powerful deity with a temper to rival the explosive nature of her gift. She was also his mother. "Ignis destroyed that abomination eons ago." Obadiah was sure of it. He would know if it still existed.

Crap. That's how they knew.

Draco had sensed his arrival because his signature was all over the damn book, thanks to his mother. Somehow they had concealed it, a powerful enchantment. Far too powerful for Draco alone.

Obadiah tuned back in when he realised Lucas was speaking again.

"Why else would you fall?"

They thought he'd learned of the book and followed the trail. If he'd known about it, the Seven would have intervened, saving Obadiah a lot of pain. He certainly wouldn't be in this mess. But how could he tell Lucas it was a knowing, that his keen intuition when it came to Zara had led to the decision? He couldn't predict the future, yet he had seen the pieces on the board and known Draco would destroy every member of the Fallen if it meant winning the war.

"If we'd known about the book, we could have put an end to this before it began." Was it so difficult for factions to communicate with one another?

"I think I might have an idea how we can locate her," Maddison said. She was moving again; not pacing this time. Now she walked with a purpose.

With a nod to Donovan, a private conversation which the rest weren't privy to, she marched out of the room.

Lucas chuckled. "You've got to love her style." He vanished a heartbeat later.

Obadiah decided to take the human route, walking the path Maddison had taken because he needed to pull his shit together.

I'm coming, Zara.

***

Maddison blinked the glare out of her eyes, the after effects of being in an enclosed space with Lucas. She knew the angel had muted his divine light, otherwise her retinas would be toast right now.

"What's the Book of Ignis?"

She turned to Donovan with a frown. "Let's just say it's a volume which should never have been written."

As they reached the bottom of the staircase, Riley walked through the door. He looked pissed.

"The son of a bitch was confident he could get in and out without effort because he certainly didn't bring back up."

Maddison smiled. "That's okay, we're taking the fight to him. How soon can you get a team together?"

Riley did an about turn back to the door. "Give me twenty."

"Shouldn't you tell him where we're going?" Donovan shuddered. "Who knows what we'll face among the Lost."

"We're all a little lost." Maddison grinned, elbowing him in the ribs. "Lighten up, D. Riley can handle himself."

Donovan muttered something under his breath, but Maddison didn't catch it. Her heart was in her mouth. It was harder than she'd anticipated to see the lifeless form of Zara's vessel.

'Maddison, what is it?' She flinched at Tobias' voice in her head, her nerves already on edge. *'Your emotional grid is all over the place.'*

'We have a situation, and if you want in, I can buy you twenty minutes before Obadiah has a total freak out and takes us all with him.'

There was a beat or two of silence. *'Draco got to Zara, didn't he?'*

'No shit, Sherlock, and he's got the kid too. Oh wait, you don't know about that part yet. Not all of it at least.' Maddison forced her feet to move until she crossed the threshold. Lucas and Sebastian were standing beside the chair, silent sentinels. Zachariah was sitting cross legged on the floor beside Zara, and Obadiah was at her back, having caught up to them. Finally. *'Just get to...'* Maddison turned to Zachariah. "What's the address?"

He recited it in a monotone, his eyes on Sebastian. It was clearly a major task to stabilise his Charge's emotions.

Maddison gave Tobias the address, moving with Obadiah to stand in front of Zara. She couldn't bring herself to drop her gaze. If she saw the vacancy in Zara's eyes she might lose it.

'Oh, and later we need to have a conversation about the blood bond you share with your Guard. If I had a similar link to Zara, I'd have her back by now.'

'You got it.'

Maddison met Obadiah's dark gaze. "If not for the spell Draco has working, Zara would be able to return to her vessel, yes?"

He nodded. "Even without the spell Zara would never leave Jeremiah, not even to get help." His eyes flashed when the implication registered.

There you go.

"But if we can somehow reverse the process, her vessel may be the answer to finding her." Maddison turned to Lucas. "Could Obadiah use the vessel? Is that even possible?"

"In theory. Yes."

"Great." Maddison winked at Obadiah. "Then what are you waiting for? Lose the meat suit and let's do this thing."

"Don't be crass, Maddy," Zachariah snapped. "Show a little respect."

I'll give you a free pass on that one.

Instead of answering Zachariah directly, she walked to pull up another chair. "Why don't you make yourself comfortable? You might not be able to switch back for a while."

Obadiah, to his credit, didn't even flinch. He sat in the chair, closed his eyes and a moment later she saw the Prime himself. He was extraordinary.

Obadiah's complexion was darker than hers, a rich olive, which highlighted the aquamarine of his eyes. And he was tall, almost as tall as Michael; his body that of strength and power.

Maddison bowed her head. "I concede your point about angel-boy." In truth the vessel looked like a child compared to Obadiah's masculine features.

He shrugged, smiling at her; the first true smile since they'd met.

Whoa.

"It's grown on me."

Maddison had to respect his easy-going nature. This was the true Obadiah. Her respect for him grew exponentially. It took strength of character to suffer as he had and not lose his humour.

She turned away when he began to glow, his light rivalling Lucas' in its sheer intensity. When she looked back, Obadiah was looking at her through her Charge's dark brown eyes.

That's some crazy shit right there.

"I think it's going to work." Obadiah closed his eyes. I can feel a…it's like a keening. A kind of gravitational pull. Zara left her print all over this body." He sounded pleased by the notion, as though it brought them closer.

Maddison glanced at Sebastian, who appeared to be fighting an emotion somewhere between hope and morbid curiosity. "I don't suppose you keep any weapons in this place?" She hadn't found any, and she'd given the house a thorough examination.

"What do you need?"

"If you're going to port them in, I could use my sword."

Sebastian placed a hand on her shoulder. No sooner had he made contact, the weapon was in her hand.

"Too cool, Seb." She turned to Donovan. "How about you? Any requests?"

Donovan pulled out two blades from the holsters beneath his jacket. "A gift from Riley. I'm good."

Maddison remembered her own gift from the wolf; a set of throwing daggers she never went anywhere without. Two of them were strapped to her thigh, the other mid-calf. She walked to the long sideboard and laid her sword across it so she could remove her coat. It would slow her down to fumble for her sword while she had it on, and there was no need for invisibility where she was going.

Donovan wandered over, taking the coat from her hand and placing it on a peg to the right of the door. By the time he returned, Maddison had her sword secured safely in the holster on her back.

When she glanced across at the others, Obadiah had Zara's quiver slung over his shoulder, her bow clutched tightly in his hand.

"Do you know how to use that thing?" she asked.

"Who do you think taught her how to use it?"

Lucas barked out a laugh. "But the student surpassed the master, a fact which surprised us all."

"It doesn't surprise me." Maddison's mind flashed to the first time they met. "Zara can work magic with that bow." Her smile faded the moment she felt the swirling mass of energy out in the yard. Everyone else felt it too. "Okay, the gang's here. Let's move out."

'Care to share the plan with me, Watcher?'

Tobias sounded tense; apprehensive, even. *'We're about to get lost, as in the Realm of the Lost. Fun. Yes?'*

The comment was met by a silence so long and deep, Maddison felt her stomach plummet. *'What is it, Tobias?'*

'It's where I served my contract.'

Maddison clutched the sideboard, pasting on a smile as the others began to file past her. Zachariah hung back, watching her steadily.

She turned to walk with him, her mind reeling. Donovan had been right. She should have mentioned the plan to Riley and Tobias. But how was she to know Tobias had spent a hundred years in darkness.

Because you didn't want to go there.

Tobias had hinted at his abuse, and yet she hadn't imagined the depravity he'd been subjected to. His mental voice said it all. Erebus, Realm of the Lost, was a barren, disconnected reality. Spending any length of time in the dark wasteland sucked away your humanity. It was a surprise he'd even survived.

Maddison stopped when she reached the exit; the first sight of him always made her pause. This time the dark energy swirled around him like a cape, as though it already had its claws in him and wanted to welcome him home.

She met his dark eyes, noticed the number of heads bowed in greeting; their respect for a king's assistance. He was the leader of the League, so every hunter would happily fight by his side.

Without taking her eyes from his, Maddison removed one of the rings from her hair. She tossed it in Tobias' direction.

'What's this?' His voice was curious. It was better than tense.

'Consider it an anchor, a token to remind you where you belong.' She realised too late how that sounded.

'And where do I belong, Watcher?'

'With your people, your family. All here are proud to stand beside you. Including me.'

Tobias bowed his head. *'Then I will wear your token with equal pride.'* He slipped it onto his finger.

SIXTEEN

Tobias fought the old, familiar demons which threatened to pull him under. Erebus was a desolate place, its land cloaked in perpetual darkness. Even Lucas' divine light was muted here.

He glanced at the Guardian, saw the shadows creeping in. It wouldn't be long before they penetrated the warm outer shell to infuse Lucas' soul with a chill it would take days to heal.

The cold recognised Tobias. It obliterated his defences and took root until he felt it bone deep.

Obadiah had led them to Dominat, a place Tobias was familiar with. The land around them was a barren wasteland; a swamp which housed the darkest souls. Standing in the centre of the land was a single-storey structure which did not belong. It had been erected from the ground itself; the soft boggy earth, hardened into a solid shell. A single door hung open to reveal a soft glow from within. The light mocked them; shone like a beacon as though in welcome to weary travellers.

"Riley and I will go in first," Maddison said, nodding to the hunter. "We all know it's a trap, and we have no choice in this. But at least I'll be able to warn you what's coming."

Tobias could feel her unease. Maddison hated going in blind, but the building was enchanted so they couldn't get a view of what awaited them. They couldn't even be sure, except for Obadiah's insistence, that Zara and Jeremiah were inside. Except for the deceptively welcoming lights, Tobias felt no sign of life. It was why Draco had chosen Dominat; it tainted everything.

'Sire. I wish you would reconsider. There's no guarantee we can protect you here.'

Tobias turned to Marcus. *'We protect each other.'* He held out his arm. Marcus clamped a large hand around his forearm without hesitation, bowing low.

Tobias repeated the pledge with Rheia and Melia, who were both in human form; both kitted out like the siren warriors of old.

"Where are his soldiers?" Sebastian said, scanning the shadows. "Why would he leave the building unprotected?"

Surprise!

A picture flashed into Tobias' head, an army of Draco's soldiers squashed together in a tiny room. It didn't help he was in the centre of the group; darkness pressing in at either side.

He turned to watch as Maddison and Riley crossed the threshold. 'If you're going to walk into a trap, take a werewolf with you.' Maddison had said that to him during their first assignment. Riley had been by her side then too.

'She's in here.' Maddison's voice was tinged with suspicion. *'Jeremiah too. They're suspended from – oh shit. Tell the angels to stay the hell out.'*

But it was too late. Obadiah, Lucas and Sebastian vanished before he could warn them. At the same instant the door slammed shut, melding with the construct of the building until it was a giant shell. There was no way in.

'Maddy?' Tobias didn't expect a response. He'd known the moment their link was severed. Without that connection to her, the darkness crept closer.

He ran a thumb along the ring on his finger, pushing away the panic. "We have to get in there. Draco's using an angel trap. Their powers are useless."

"Son of a bitch." Zachariah looked about ready to pull the building apart with his bare hands.

"Guys."

They both turned at the warning in Donovan's tone. Dozens of wraiths were creeping from the marsh, their eyes soulless, their mouths open in a soundless scream.

Tobias pulled his daggers free, calculating the odds as he glanced at his crew. There were nine of them against an army. It would not be an easy fight. He turned to Zachariah with a grin. "I don't suppose you can throw some of you happy juice at them and make them a little friendlier?"

It earned him an eye-roll. "They don't have the capacity to feel. They lost that a long time ago."

"I can't control them, you can't charm them, so it looks like we're about to dance." Tobias ran forward to where Donovan was already fighting off a deadly trio.

The wraiths were corporeal, so at least it was an even playing field. That said, their long, clawed fingers gave them a slight advantage.

He fought back to back with Donovan as what seemed like an endless stream of creatures came at them; drawn by the scent of their blood. There was no time to check his injuries, or the progress of his team. Tobias had to trust that if they needed it, the others would call for help.

It was oddly soundless, their battle. The wraiths carried no weapons, they didn't need any. It was the shadows; a fog which curled around their feet and stole all signs of life until they were surrounded by nothing. Such was the power of Dominat. Tobias couldn't even hear his own breathing, though he knew it was laboured.

Alarm bells rang in his head. The cries of those in need would be sucked into the abyss. He wouldn't hear them. If his people needed him, he wouldn't hear a thing. So he used the other part of his power and stepped out of his conscious body to look down on the action below.

One of the hunters, a male from Riley's group, was struggling to disengage a wraith who had attached itself to his back. The thing had its claws hooked into the hunter's sides, its mouth open in a silent scream of triumph.

Tobias dropped back down and gave Donovan a heads up before cutting a path to where the hunter now lay, writhing on the ground. He sliced his blade through the wraiths arm, using two daggers at once. Satisfied he was free, Tobias turned too late to avoid a blow to his arm. He felt his flesh tear, smelled the aroma of blood, and knew he was in trouble.

Backing away from the hunter, Tobias turned in a circle as six wraiths glided toward him.

***

Maddison gripped the makeshift post, clenching her muscles in a way which mimicked Riley beside her. She hoped Draco would buy the ruse, continuing to believe his entrapment had worked. The others were strung from the roof, each of their chains attached to an angel trap carved into the surface of the inner shell. It was clever, she couldn't fault Draco for his planning skills. The angels were powerless; as weak as kittens. She was on her own for the moment.

She glanced across at Riley, saw the beast behind his eyes was all but clawing to get out. Riley had a powerful mind, and she knew from experience Draco's tricks would not hold him for long.

Her eyes narrowed on Orion Reece, who was shoulder to shoulder with Draco, his face an inscrutable mask.

What is your game?

Clearly Orion was keeping secrets from his so-called leader. He knew how powerful Maddison was, and about her immunity to control based magic. Yet Draco was oblivious. He didn't view her as any kind of threat. She would use that to her advantage.

The leader of the Fractured was unusually quiet. His big, heavy bulk was bent over the alter he'd erected, intent on his task. He meant to use the angels to power his army. Perhaps it had been his plan all along.

'Exactly how much control do you have over that hair?'

Maddison didn't look at Obadiah, she kept her eyes focused on the action in front of her. *'Exactly how much power do you have?'* He shouldn't be able to path to her, since the angel trap took away his abilities. Not to mention the cloaking spells Maddison could taste like hot spice on her tongue.

'Currently? Very little. But I grow stronger with each passing day.' There was a note of impatience.

'Maybe we can negotiate a rain check. Draco appears to be in a good mood.'

In truth, Maddison had expected a lot more than a back-hander for her stunt the last time they met. She had waited for Draco to unleash his frustration, relished the thought of going toe to toe with him. A split lip was all she got, which, granted, hurt like a bitch.

'There's a ring in my right pocket. If you could reach it, somehow get it to Jeremiah, we might stand a chance of getting out of here alive.'

Maddison searched through her memories until she found what she was looking for. Aretha's voice echoed in her head. *'Ensure the outcast is wearing this before they drain him completely. It will bind him to me.'*

'It would be my pleasure.' She had to bite down on the smile. It was time to have a little fun.

"You know, Draco. I'm surprised you don't have more backup," she said conversationally, catching his attention. "Were you so convinced your little tricks were going to work?"

"I don't need any help to crush you, witch, and if I did, I have the loyalty of a god."

Are you sure about that?

Draco stepped away from the alter to walk over to her, drawn by his arrogance.

"Ah, but the thing is, even gods have their weakness."

Draco's eyes narrowed. She didn't miss the shadow of doubt. "You think you can take on a god?" He laughed, turning to Orion. "Is your ego really that inflated?"

"I'm good." Maddison winked, purposely taunting him. "But I'm not that good."

"She's up to something." Orion stepped up to her, his expression neutral. It was as though they had never met.

Her smile grew, a big, false smile she hoped they would see through. "I'm also a curious sort, and I discovered your pet god here has an equally powerful father. You know the stories of Nox don't you?"

"What's she talking about?" Draco snapped, growing bored with the conversation. "Knock her out. I may have use for her later."

Maddison laughed, a grating high-pitched sound that made Riley's wolf growl. "Those were my thoughts exactly." She looked Orion in the eyes. "This is nothing personal, you understand."

"What-"

"Dormio requies."

Orion crumpled to the floor like someone had removed his batteries.

"That's impossible." Draco's voice was shrill, furious. He put his hands around Maddison's throat. "Wake him. Now."

Anger burned along her skin, igniting the band she wore around her neck. Draco released her immediately. But only so he would gather his power.

Maddison didn't give him the chance. Her hair whipped out, the braid extending to curl round and round his body; pinning his arms to his sides.

Her silken bonds didn't hold. Draco's power pushed against her own, forcing her to relax her hold.

She spun to Riley, slapping her hand over his heart and looking him dead in the eye. "Now."

Maddison stepped back as Riley exploded into wolf form, his howl terrifying in the small room.

Draco opened a portal and four wraiths drifted out, hungry for blood.

Riley headed them off and Draco hurried back to his alter, while Maddison extended her hair and flicked it toward Obadiah. A jolt of feedback shot along her braid when she made contact with Aretha's ring. It packed quite a punch.

She snagged the ring in her hand as her mane whipped out to strike the wraith bearing down on her. His claws grazed her arm, but didn't penetrate the suit; the angle was wrong.

Maddison grabbed one of her daggers in her left hand, grateful the ugly little bastards were in corporeal form. She vaulted across to where Jeremiah hung suspended from the ceiling and jabbed the ring on his finger.

"Hang in there, kid," she whispered.

"Very funny."

His mumbled response made her laugh, a soft sound drowned out by pitiless screeching a second before one of the wraiths landed on her back. Maddison stumbled, her hair winding itself around the wraith's body as she tried to yank the damn thing off. It clung on, sinking its claws into her shoulders and drawing blood.

Ah, oh.

Maddison spun, re-evaluating her earlier decision to remove the coat. It would come in handy right about now. A lance of pain seared down her arm as the wraith gripped tighter. She shot a jolt of raw energy into her braid, satisfied when she heard the wraith scream.

"Maddy! Look out."

At Zara's warning, she turned again, spinning in a tight circle. The second wraith hit her from the side, knocking her off her feet. Maddison collided with the alter, scattering the items across the floor.

"No." Draco grabbed the wraith still attached to her back and pulled. She screamed as the creature's claws tore her flesh. But she was finally free.

"Get down."

Maddison dropped and rolled, barely avoiding Draco's blast.
'Thanks.'

Obadiah nodded, looking up at the roof. *'You might want to stay down. And cover your head.'*

'Why? What-'

Maddison's breath came out in a rush as the walls around her burst into flame. The roof went up in smoke, burning so quickly her brain struggled to process what had happened. The Fae Queen was fast. Maddison didn't look up, but she knew from the long, dark shadow, Aretha was there. Her first impulse was to steal a glance at the fiery dragon, until she realised the purpose of Aretha's intervention. To destroy the angel trap. Instinctively, Maddison covered her head; or, more accurately, her eyes, when Lucas lit up like a nuclear power plant.

She counted to ten, waited for the glow to die down, and peered out at the scene from beneath her arm. The first thing she saw was Orion's prone form. He had a cut along his cheek about seven inches long. It was deep too, judging from the amount of blood.

You owe him.

Maddison crawled over to him and pushed her braid beneath his body to fashion a loose rope. He was a heavy son of a bitch, but she managed to crawl through the debris, pulling him behind her. She had no idea where she was headed, she only knew her head was spinning and a few dozen more of Draco's minions were circling above.

"Where do you think you're going?"

Maddison froze at Draco's voice. He sounded royally pissed and she couldn't blame him. They had brought the building down on top of his plans.

Draco bent to pick her up by the arms. Her hair retracted, releasing Orion to whip out at the new threat. Draco dropped her to her feet, his face morphing until he was more serpent than man.

"Maddy. Duck!"

She hit the deck at Lucas' command, pain lancing a hole in her brain. But it wasn't from the impact. It was from the scream tearing through her mind, a sound of intense suffering. It was Tobias. He was in trouble.

SEVENTEEN

Zara shot wave after wave of energy into the wraiths, who were hell bent on snacking on Jeremiah. She didn't have her weapons, so she had to use her power. The empathic ability had no effect; these creatures were already so lost they felt nothing but an automated sense of loyalty to the darkness.

She dropped down in front of Jeremiah, and together they fought them back; Jeremiah using what looked suspiciously like a table leg. Obadiah had his hands full too, though he was holding his own. It was still a shock to look upon her own vessel instead of the face which was becoming all too familiar to her.

Obadiah's gaze was on the sky, where Aretha, in her dragon skin, was setting the sky on fire as she battled a handful of wraiths. Zara couldn't take her eyes from Obadiah, no matter how extraordinary Aretha was. Something had changed in him, and it wasn't the new body. He was growing in power.

As if to demonstrate that, Obadiah opened his arms wide in a move she instantly recognised, bringing his palms together with a resounding smack. The remaining soldiers dropped as though someone had cut their strings. The only downside to his ability was that their team were vulnerable too.

Zara spotted Riley, still in wolf form, lying on his side. He wasn't completely out, but the blast had winded him. Other hunters were down too. She couldn't see her brother, but knew he was already attending to the wounded. Donovan was one of them. It was Sebastian's job to get them to safety.

Lucas and Draco were still battling it out, the sound of their anger rippled like thunder. Just as it appeared neither of them would gain the upper hand, Lucas hit Draco with a lightning bolt of pure energy and Draco went down in the dirt.

"A little help here."

Zara turned to Obadiah, who was crouched beside the splintered alter. He had the Book of Ignis in his hands. "How will you destroy it?"

He smiled so quickly Zara figured it was a response to something one of the others had said. She glanced at the sky, saw Aretha circling above them. If Zara wasn't mistaken, the long, sleek jaws were pulled back into a horrific grin.

"Let's see what putting this through the fae burner will do," Obadiah said, holding the book low to the ground.

"Ha!" Zara followed the book's progress as Obadiah launched it into the air. Aretha didn't miss a beat, she roared, sending a white hot burst of flame across the sky. Zara felt the heat from the ground.

An explosion shattered the darkness above, a multitude of colour so bright it stung.

"Damn you." Draco turned, his scaly face crimson. The fury exploded out of him, sending Lucas back ten feet.

Lucas sat up, stunned. The hesitation cost them. Draco summoned a portal and stepped in, taking Orion Reece with him.

"Well that was-" Zara gasped at the violent shudder beneath her feet. Her mouth dropped open in surprise when she saw the culprit. The Book of Ignis lay on the ground, surprisingly undamaged despite the power of the Fae Queen.

Aretha landed beside it, transforming in a burst of fiery red. "Any suggestions?" Her eyes were on Lucas, not Obadiah.

Zara understood why an instant later. Two members of the Alliance flanked him.

***

It was dark. Dark and cold, so very cold. Tobias was lost in a sea of nothing, his thoughts splintered, his heart a hard pit in his chest. And yet something tugged at him, weighed him down, when all he wanted was to float into oblivion.

He reached out with his mind, floating above himself to look down on the scene below with an odd sense of detachment. He'd been put through the ringer, there were cuts and bruises all over his body. The wraiths, he remembered. There had been so damn many.

Maddison was checking his wounds. Her face was pale, but he didn't know if it was worry or the result of blood loss, because she had a pretty nasty gash herself. That got his heart pumping again, though the outrage was fleeting; swallowed up by apathy. His new friend.

She was talking to him but he couldn't hear the words. Perhaps he didn't want to hear. Maddison's thoughts were battering around in his brain, her mental voice jumbled. She wasn't making any sense.

Tobias started to sink back into the comforting nothingness, it was a familiar place. A powerful place. But a sharp pain in his right hand stopped him in his tracks. Maddison had his fingers in hers. She was stroking the ring she had given him, making it impossible for him to slide away.

He watched, fascinated, moved by the beauty of her fierce expression. He felt the warmth, a subtle energy which overlaid the cold chambers of his heart.

Maddison grabbed his head, turning it with more care than he'd expected. From his position, he looked in the direction she wanted him to face, and saw Marcus for the first time. He was out cold.

Anger flooded his system, pulling his mind back. He sucked in a breath, startled by the explosion of sound when he settled back into consciousness. "What happened?" His voice was barely recognisable.

"I don't know." Maddison held her hands above his chest. "There's a wraith inside you." Her eyes grew wide. "You have to expel it, Tobias. You have to cast it out."

A memory flashed into his mind; one of the creatures hitting him in the centre of his chest and then, nothing. Nothing but the cold.

This time he used his gift to look inward, saw the wraith burrowing into his mind, and understood it was gaining power. It would take everything he had to give and leave him empty; a heartless, barren shell.

He knew how it had gotten in. This place wanted him. It weakened him both physically and mentally. The wraith had seen an opening and taken it. "Listen, Maddy. You have to help me break the blood bond. If I fail, I take them with me. I won't allow-"

Maddison stole his words with a kiss, stole his breath, and his desire to lay down and die. *'You're stronger than this, damn you.'* It was almost a shout. *'Get your head out of your ass and show that son of a bitch what you're made of.'*

Tobias felt his mind spark, his power uncurl inside him in a long lazy stretch. It felt good, the hum of energy reaching every inch of his skin, even his lips.

No. That's all Maddy.

With a grin, he focused his power; allowing it to expand to every corner of his being, until there was nowhere left for the wraith to go. Except out.

Tobias felt the moment he was free of the parasite. Maddison felt it too because she began to chant, her words low and powerful. When he opened his eyes it was to see Maddison driving a dagger through the wraith's chest.

She shrugged when he raised his eyebrows at her. "Clearly, he didn't understand the consequences of challenging a king."

Tobias wanted to laugh, but found he didn't have the energy. He settled for a smile. A smile which broadened when he heard Marcus rouse in his head.

'Sire. Are you okay?'

'I will be.' Tobias closed his eyes, drifting again, only this time it was sleep waiting to claim him.

"How we doing over here?"

Tobias didn't open his eyes, or answer Sebastian's question. He didn't need to.

"The king needs rest. Can you transport us to the palace?"

He missed the response, his mind was full of Maddison. He had come to expect it. This distraction he felt with his witch.

Careful. She isn't yours.

The next thing Tobias became aware of, was the familiar feel of his bed as Marcus settled him against the mattress. He was home.

'Sleep well, half-blood.' Maddison's words echoed in his mind.

'Thank you, Watcher. I owe you one.'

Her snort came through loud and clear, and he discovered he had the strength to laugh after all. He drifted into slumber with a smile on his lips and a witch on his mind.

***

Zara tuned out when the council began talking about the book. She knew what their presence meant; the Alliance had come to take Obadiah home. Her mind began to wander, observing the group with the barest level of interest. The senior council member, Kayde, was with Jeremiah, talking in a soothing tone Zara couldn't hear, but which grated along her nerves.

Kayde walked across to her, his expression gentle. "It's time to say your goodbyes."

She felt a wave of panic and glanced at Obadiah to see he now held the book in what appeared to be a glass box. How had she missed that? He met her eyes, and though they were the soft hazel which belonged to her vessel, she saw only the aquamarine of his true gaze. They burned into her until her own eyes began to water.

"I have to go now."

Zara spun to Jeremiah, who looked so young despite his true age. "Have they told you what will happen?" she asked, trying to keep the tears at bay.

"No. But I'm not afraid, Zara the Fair."

She did cry then, pulling him into her arms and holding on tight. "You remembered."

"No. Not yet. But it felt like something I should say."

"I'm sorry, Jerry. I want you to know I'm so sorry I forgot us." Zara stood back when it registered he was laughing. "What's so funny?"

"That you stole my name." He winked at her, and there he was. Jeremiah in all his glory. "I think you remembered more than you think." He nodded over her shoulder, indicating they had company.

Zara knew who it was. It was time to say goodbye to Obadiah. Her body turned despite the denial in her heart. How could she let him go?

"Will they take my memories again?" she asked, conscious of their audience. Part of her hoped he would say yes.

"Do you want them to?" Obadiah's eyes smiled into hers because he knew of such temptation. He had to.

"No."

"Liar."

Zara laughed and wiped her tears. "How much trouble are you in?"

"Trouble? They'll probably give me a medal. We won this round." He reached to tuck a strand of hair behind her ear.

"Did we?"

"Mostly." He bowed to concede the point. "Whatever the punishment, it was worth it to see you again."

Zara's throat closed up. She didn't want to say the words. They were too hard. "Thank you." She switched to her mental voice. *'Thank you for doing what you promised.'*

'I will always be there for you.' They were the words he had uttered hundreds of years ago. A vow he had stood by. *'You are my heart and my soul. Remember that.'*

He turned to nod at the others. Zara slumped forward when she saw his light leave her vessel. She would have dropped to the ground, her agony too great, if Lucas hadn't caught her around the waist.

"Oh, Luke."

He hugged her to him, cradling her head against his chest. "Let me help you, little one."

Zara shook her head. The simple fact was, when it came down to it, she would rather deal with the loss than forget him again. She stood, gathering herself when she felt Maddison's energy approaching. Now was not the time to wallow in self-pity. There would be an opportunity to grieve later, when they had finished what they started.

Lucas released her, kissing the top of her head the way he used to when they were children. "The Alliance chose wisely," he said to Maddison.

"If you're thanking me for saving your ass in there, I'd say I owe half of the glory to Aretha." Maddison glanced around in disappointment. "Who I was hoping to meet."

As Lucas gave Maddison a lecture on minding her manners, Zara stepped into her vessel. The echo of Obadiah soothed her, focused her in the present. There was still one more thing left to do.

"We need to locate Jeremiah's blood and destroy it," she said, staring down at the broken vial on the floor. Bending, she picked it up. "Is this enough for a location spell?"

Maddison took it from her. "It's enough." She turned to Lucas. "If I may be so bold. You need to find a way to protect the remaining outcasts. I don't think Draco will attempt to leash the Fallen again, but they're still at risk."

"Is there anything else we should be doing?" Lucas' lips twitched.

"Actually, I want to look into a blood bond, which will connect the Fallen to their Watchers."

Zara choked out a laugh. "I can't believe you just said that. Six months ago you avoided any kind of connection, and now you're willing to bind yourself to me?"

Maddison narrowed her eyes. "You're right. What am I thinking?" She pulled a face, one Zara was all too familiar with. "You're clearly a bad influence."

"Clearly." Zara hugged her. She knew Maddison wouldn't thank her for the display of affection. It simply felt like the right thing to do.

After a brief moment of awkward silence, Maddison cleared her throat. She stepped to the remnants of the alter and stabbed it into the ground.

Zara's gaze dropped to the vial, still in Maddison's hand. As Maddison began to chant softly, the microscopic fibres in the glass burst to life; glowing an effervescent red. The alter vibrated in the ground and a map appeared to carve itself into the grain; a section of the mortal realm drawn by an invisible hand. She recognised the pattern immediately. It was central London.

"Show me," Maddison murmured, releasing the vial. It smashed against the alter, and fine droplets began to gather in a spot at the top right hand corner of the map.

"There." Maddison weaved a little on her feet. It wasn't until that moment Zara noticed the dried blood on her neck.

"You're injured."

Maddison waved it off. "I'm fine." Her gaze shot to Lucas, who was studying the map. "Do you want back up?"

Lucas bowed low, and Zara knew he was hiding a smile. "I think I'll manage." Then he was gone.

"So that's it?" Maddison stared at the map. "It's over?"

"For now." She held out her hand. "What do you say we go home? I think we both earned a little rest."

"We deserve to get cleaned up at least." Maddison glanced down at her shoulder. "I think I got blood on my suit again." She put her hand in Zara's. "Maybe I should send Draco my dry cleaning bill."

Zara laughed lightly because she knew it was what Maddison wanted. She also knew she'd have a fight on her hands just to get a moment alone. Maddison had always been able to read her, and whether she admitted it or not, her greatest gift was her heart. Sometimes she cared too much.

EIGHTEEN

Obadiah fought back a wave of anxiety; a beast that clawed at his chest like a caged animal. He was tired of waiting for the council to decide his fate, and, in truth, he was unaccustomed to being at this side of the inner sanctum. He should be in there; he was one of the Seven. But it was his transgression his brothers and sisters now discussed. Obadiah had no choice but to toe the line, to consider the possibility he might lose his right to serve among them.

In some ways it was good to be home. His powers were back to full strength, and he couldn't deny the peace which soothed his aching heart. Yet he would trade it all to be with Zara; his powers, his position, his place in the world.

He flinched when the outer door opened, startled when he realised who it was. "Mother." Obadiah dropped to one knee in front of her.

"What am I to do with you, Obadiah?" she said, her tone gentle.

"I ask only that I am allowed to keep my memories." He looked up, into eyes the colour of burnt autumn leaves.

"Look where that got us the last time." Ignis' face creased into a frown as she considered his request.

"Please, mother. I-"

She held up a hand. "If we'd been able to wipe your memories, don't you think we'd have done so by now?" Her fingers twitched, giving him permission to stand. "Your ties to her are too great. I've watched you mourn year after year and it broke my heart."

Obadiah bowed his head. "I'm sorry for causing you pain."

"Do you know what a privilege it is to be a Prime?" Ignis made a sweeping gesture when he would have spoken. "We need you, Obadiah. As you well know, a war is coming. It will have far reaching consequences."

"I never meant to turn my back on my duties, but they needed me, mother."

She walked across to him, cupped his cheek with her hand. Her touch was surprisingly cool, considering the flames he saw dancing in her eyes. "What would you say if I told you we have prepared for this inevitable battle for centuries? That we have agents in the mortal realm, good soldiers who help to even the score?"

"I'd say that sounds inevitable too. We have too many rules, where the darkness have none."

Ignis shook her head. "Don't be naive, son. Those rules might be self-serving, but they exist. And sometimes rules are meant to be broken."

"You knew I would fall?" Why had he not seen it before? His journey had been too easy, his path unobstructed by the Alliance. They had allowed him his freedom.

"I was counting on it." She bent to kiss his cheek.

"What happens now?"

His mother glanced toward the door, where the group were still deliberating his fate. "Now we wait to hear what they decide."

An hour later, as he walked the halls of Ignis Tower, Obadiah still couldn't believe the verdict. Even after his mother had admitted the truth, he'd expected to be punished. Nothing could have been worse than losing Zara again, so he had been resigned to his fate. Now he didn't know what to think. He was afraid to believe. Afraid to hope.

For the love of the gods, you're a Prime. Act like it.

"Lecturing yourself again?"

He almost collided with Jeremiah, and it was Jeremiah the angel he knew and loved like his own kin.

They embraced on a laugh. "I missed you, my friend." Obadiah didn't care that his voice broke.

"I'd say I missed you too." Jeremiah stepped back, tapping his forehead with his index finger. "But for me it's only been a few hours."

He hadn't thought of it before, but Maddison had the same dry wit and smart mouth. They could have been related. It made Obadiah smile, explained why Zara was so drawn to her.

"So is that it? Is your sentence over?" he asked as they fell into an easy rhythm and began to walk.

"Yes. Finally! I have a new assignment." Jeremiah grinned. "I'm joining the ranks of the Fallen. Well, not exactly. Since I was born in the mortal realm I don't actually have to fall. But I get my powers back, so I guess that makes me unique."

"Arrogant too. We can't forget that."

Obadiah turned to glance at his friend's profile; his pale skin, the pale hair. Damn, but he'd missed the kid. "What's the new assignment?"

"Would you believe my mortal father?" Jeremiah shook his head. "I never thought I'd see him again. Not after my mother finally kicked him out, but it appears we're about to be reacquainted."

Gregory's father had been a soldier. He suffered with PTSD after the Demonic War and left the service shortly afterwards. That much Obadiah got from Zara.

"But first I get to spend time with our girl." He grinned, his face lit with excitement. "I'm told there will be a period of adjustment as my new powers adjust to the restrictions of my human form."

"So, basically, what you're saying is, that you're not so different from the Fallen after all."

"Details, my friend. Details."

Obadiah rolled his eyes toward the grand, crystal roof of the tower. It was going to be fun watching his friend earn his stripes in the mortal realm. In fact, he was looking forward to it.

***

Zara waited a beat before entering Bob's apartment. She felt her brother's presence inside, and knew Bob's time was near. It was almost as though he'd waited for her.

She faltered when she saw him. He was in so much pain, but trying to mask it as always.

"There she is," he said on a wheezing cough. "I've been worried about you, young 'un."

To Bob she was Gloria, and that was the way it had to stay. So she pasted on a sassy smile and walked further into the room. "That bug got me bad. It put me on my back for days." She took the seat opposite him, feeing the lie lance at her conscience. "I'm sorry I missed our date."

He snorted. "You have better options than a sick, old man."

"That's not how I see you." Zara didn't hide the sheen of tears. "I'm your friend."

Bob smiled, a beautiful smile she felt in her very soul. "You've been good to me these last few years."

"As you have been good to me."

"It's almost a shame I have to go. But it's my time, Gloria."

Zara dropped to her knees in front of him and gripped his hand. "I understand." Her smile was wet. "But I'm going to miss you."

Bob closed his eyes, wincing against the pain. Out of habit, Zara took from him what she could. She turned when she felt a hand on her shoulder. Sebastian smiled kindly, bowing his head in silent salute. He had volunteered to collect Bob's soul for her. Part of her brother's duties were still that of Gatekeeper.

'I'll take care of him, sister.'

"Okay." Zara closed her eyes and dropped her head onto Bob's hand. She felt the moment his soul left his body, and she accepted the piece of her he took with him.

She sat that way for several long minutes, even when the pain began to recede; hers and Bob's. It was a long way back to her apartment. Zara felt sick with grief. This time it wouldn't pass. Her Ward wasn't the only one she was grieving for.

Her body froze on the threshold, confused by the energy she sensed beyond the door. It couldn't be.

Zara's heart expanded like a balloon when she entered to find Obadiah waiting patiently for her. There were no barriers between them now; he held nothing back. Zara felt it all; the love, the joy, the passion.

She ran to him, jumping into his arms and clinging to the wonderful strength of him. His lips were hungry on hers, so firm and demanding.

Zara laughed as they broke apart. "Please don't tell me you broke the rules again already."

He grinned. "Not exactly. This time I'm following orders." Obadiah dropped her to the ground to take her hand. "But before I get into that, I have another surprise for you."

She followed him to the guest room, giddy with relief he was whole and unharmed.

"Barriers up, or it will spoil the surprise," Obadiah said, pausing in the hall.

She complied without question, happier than she had any right to be. She should have known what waited for her behind the guest room door; Obadiah's expression said it all. Yet when she saw Jeremiah stretched out on the bed her joy bubbled over.

"What does this mean?" Zara swiped at the tears but they kept coming, especially when she felt the buzz of Jeremiah's unique signature permeating the room. He already belonged.

"It means Jerry has joined the ranks of the Fallen, and he gets a secret identity."

"Gregory."

"Gregory."

Zara laughed at the way their minds were in tune, and the piece that had been missing, the hole she could never explain, filled with her love for these two angels.

"And you?" she asked, backing out of the room so Jeremiah could rest.

"Me? I'm an agent of the Seven. I get to work in both camps."

"They're letting you stay?" It was almost too good to be true. There had to be a catch.

"Until the war is over, yes." He wrapped his arms around her. "After that. Who knows? I've never been too fond of rules anyway."

EPILOGUE

Maddison paced the floor of her room. She felt edgy, anxious even, though she had no idea why. They had won the round, but there were still loose ends. They niggled at her, tormented her until her nerves were so frayed she jumped at the slightest sound.

Lack of sleep was the culprit. She hadn't slept in two days, which made her hell to be around. It was the reason her friends were avoiding her. Even Donovan had made himself scarce.

Heat prickled along her skin, warning her what was coming. Instead of irritation, she felt only relief.

Orion appeared in an explosion of light, still less fanfare than she was used to, but a bigger bang than before.

Gods help me, but I was worried about him.

"Woody, I'm so glad to see you're still in one piece."

"What did I tell you about calling me that?" Her tone was more forceful than she intended, especially as she was getting used to that too.

"Somebody needs their beauty sleep." Orion wiggled his fingers. "Want some help with that?"

"Thank you, but I can handle it. What do you want, Orion?"

"I came to compliment you on your performance, and to thank you for not blowing my cover."

Maddison waited for the dig, for the other shoe to drop, but he was completely serious.

"Exactly what kind of game are you playing?" It was disconcerting. If this continued, she might actually grow to like him.

"If I told you that it would spoil my fun." He smiled at her, and it was so close to a genuine smile she felt the urge to lie down.

"You enjoy messing with my head, don't you?"

Orion's dark eyes flashed with amusement. "It's one of my favourite past times." He walked over to the long window and looked out onto the fountain below. With a flick of his wrist, the water began to dance. It irked her that she enjoyed to do the same thing. She didn't want to have anything in common with him.

"Tell me, Maddison. How did you know I was born from the night? I've never shared that with anybody."

Oh great. Here it comes.

"It was a lucky guess, powered by the magic of the internet. What's wrong, did I get you in trouble?"

Orion turned, pensive all of a sudden. "On the contrary. It worked like a charm." He moved so quickly he was in front of her before she could blink. "Stay safe out there, Woody. I'll be in touch."

He was gone, stealing her opportunity to tell him to go to hell. The worst of it was, part of her was relieved he hadn't been hurt. The last time she'd seen him he'd been about as defenceless as any god was liable to get.

'Will you get some sleep? Your anxiety is like white noise in my head.'

She smiled at Tobias' petulant tone. *'Your Majesty. How are you feeling?'*

'I've been better.'

It hit her then, the real reason she was consumed by restless energy. She was worried about him too. *'Do you feel up to a guest?'*

Tobias was silent for so long she thought he might refuse. *'I'm...still recuperating. I haven't been feeling myself.'*

Maddison frowned at the embarrassment in his tone. He was worried she would see it as a weakness. *'You did take a few good licks out there.'* She tried to keep her mental voice casual. It probably wasn't a good idea to go to him. But until she knew he was okay, saw it with her own eyes, there would be no rest. *'But don't worry. I have a solution for what ails you.'*

'Hmm, I like the sound of that.'

She laughed, already on the move. *'Get your mind out of the gutter, Your Majesty. Though it has to be said I have a magic touch.'*

Maddison was hoping to avoid Marcus. She needed sleep before facing his particular band of torture. She felt bitchy and mean, not a good combination when facing the shapeshifter. They already rubbed each other the wrong way.

Of course it was just her luck he would meet her at the damn door.

"Marcus, what a pleasant surprise."

He ignored her sarcasm and looked down at the flask in her hand. "Tell me that's something to help him sleep. I've tried everything."

The news Tobias wasn't sleeping shocked the hell out of her, but she recovered quickly. "It'll make him sleep like a baby."

Marcus stood back so she could enter, clearly Tobias wasn't any fun to live with either when he needed rest. The thought pleased her.

It was a testament to how frayed Marcus' nerves were that he didn't so much as look in her direction until they arrived at the royal suite. He even resisted the urge to morph, perhaps afraid she would pour her miracle soup over his head.

Without a word, he pushed the doors open and marched back the way he had come.

Tobias was sitting up in a bed so big it was its own room. He had his back against several plush pillows, the bare skin of his broad shoulders contrasting; a rich liquid brown.

Get a grip, Maddy.

"You look like crap," she said, glancing at the bruises on his hands and face.

"But you have a solution for that. Don't you, Watcher." He patted the bed beside him, blue eyes flashing with challenge.

Maddison waved the flask at him. "Secret family recipe." She accepted the challenge, sitting as close to him as she dared. "The Thorne family to be exact. Triston used to feed us this when we got sick."

"Zachariah's father, right?" he asked as she poured the soup.

"Yes. He swears by it." She offered him the cup, watching him warily.

Tobias took the cup, raising it to his lips; his eyes on hers. The look was so intense Maddison dropped her gaze.

Her attention landed on the ring she'd given him. It looked too thin on his large hand; the long elegant fingers dwarfed the band. She couldn't resist reaching out to touch the metal. When she removed her finger, the ring reflected its wearer. A thick band which flattened at the centre, stamped with the royal crest.

Tobias stared down at it, his expression curious. "You know what it means when a woman gives a man a ring?" His eyes danced with mischief.

"No. What does it mean?" Her heart accelerated. They were on dangerous territory, and her every instinct was to run.

He grinned. "It means you like me."

"Meh." She smiled too, and wiggled her hand.

Tobias' smile grew wider as he continued to drink the soup. He remained silent, finishing every drop. "Thank you for the ring." His eyes dropped to the crest. "It did its job." Handing her the cup he settled further back into the cushions. "Now, why don't you tell me what's keeping that busy brain of yours awake?"

You.

Maddison kicked off her boots and crossed her legs to sit more comfortably on the bed. This she could handle. She enjoyed talking to him about her day. Granted, she didn't normally do that in his bedroom. But she could make an exception.

She told him about Obadiah's return, about her visit from Orion, letting it all pour out in a stream of words. When she was done she felt better, certainly less tense than before. Her body finally began to relax.

Maddison looked across at Tobias, surprised that at some point during their conversation he had fallen asleep. She sat for a moment, looking at the hard lines of his handsome face. A lock of dark hair had fallen across his forehead. She couldn't resist smoothing it away.

With a smile, she kissed her fingertips, and pressed them softly to his lips. "Sleep well, Your Majesty."

Gathering her boots, and the flask, she crept out of the room. She didn't see anyone until Marcus appeared to show her out, his brows raised in surprise when she grinned at him.

"You're welcome."

She left Marcus standing on the threshold staring after her. It was extremely satisfying.

Maddison took the quickest route to Merc Hall, ignoring everyone she passed.

Dropping her boots at the door, she all but jogged to her bed and dove between the sheets. The soft comforter felt like a warm caress when she removed the suit.

'Sleep well, Watcher.'

She turned out the lights with a flick of her wrist, and fell into a dreamless sleep with a smile on her face.

Connect with Melissa Barker-Simpson

I hope you enjoyed The Fallen. Thanks for reading! If you'd like to connect, here's how:

Friend me on Facebook:

http://facebook.com/mbarkersimpson

Follow me on Twitter:

http://twitter.com/mbarkersimpson

Subscribe to my blog:

http://www.mbarkersimpson.wordpress.com

Visit my website:

http://www.mbarkersimpson.co.uk

Printed in Great Britain
by Amazon